Other books in the same series

THE ROYAL RABBITS OF LONDON

THE ROYAL RABBITS OF LONDON:
ESCAPE FROM THE TOWER

THE ROYAL RABBITS OF LONDON:
THE GREAT DIAMOND CHASE

# THE ROYAL RABBITS OF LONDON

## THE HUNT FOR THE GOLDEN CARROT

### SANTA MONTEFIORE · SIMON SEBAG MONTEFIORE

ILLUSTRATED BY KATE HINDLEY

First published in Great Britain in 2019 by Simon & Schuster UK Ltd
A CBS COMPANY

1 3 5 7 9 10 8 6 4 2

Simon & Schuster UK Ltd
1ˢᵗ Floor, 222 Gray's Inn Road
London
WC1X 8HB


www.simonandschuster.co.uk

Simon & Schuster Australia, Sydney
Simon & Schuster India, New Delhi

A CIP catalogue record for this book is available from the British Library.

HB ISBN: 978-1-4711-7150-5
eBook ISBN:978-1-4711-7151-2

Printed and bound by CPI Group (UK) Ltd, Croydon, CR0 4YY

MIX
Paper from
responsible sources
FSC® C020471

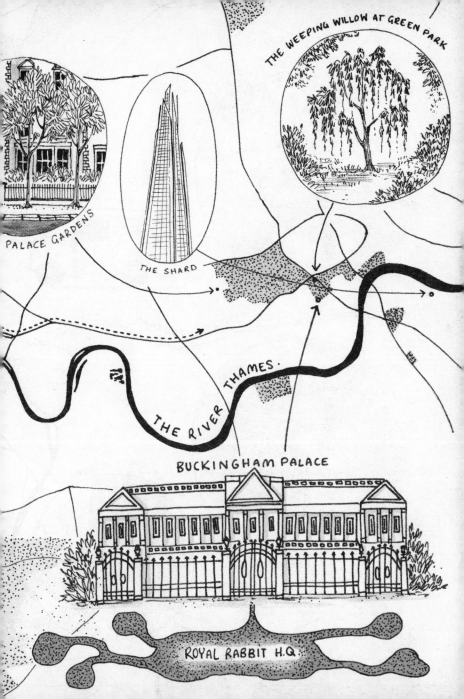

THE WEEPING WILLOW AT GREEN PARK

PALACE GARDENS

THE SHARD

THE RIVER THAMES.

BUCKINGHAM PALACE

ROYAL RABBIT H.Q.

# THE RABBIT KINGDOM

**buck**  male rabbit

**bunkin**  country rabbit

**bunny**  young rabbit

**doe**  female rabbit

**Hopster**  large, strong and clever rabbit

**Thumper**  Special Forces
commando rabbit

# CHAPTER ONE

Deep beneath the state rooms of Buckingham Palace, in the secret headquarters of the Royal Rabbits of London, Shylo awoke with a start. He didn't rub his eyes sleepily as he usually did and he didn't yawn. He sat bolt upright as if his little body had been seized by an electric shock.

'Today I'm going home!' he cried with excitement, jumping up on the mattress and breaking into an excited dance. He bounced up and down so energetically that his big, floppy ears flapped about

his head like clumsy wings. 'Today I'm going *ho-ome*! Today I'm going *ho-ome*!' he sang, kicking out his big feet and wiggling his fluffy tail.

It was late summer, and Shylo hadn't seen his mother since the spring. The thought of being with her again filled him with happiness. The little bunkin had left his home in haste to warn the Royal Rabbits of a plot to harm the Queen, and there had been no time to say goodbye to any of his family. He never imagined that a weak and feeble bunny like him would then be invited to join the elite organization of rabbits who were sworn to protect the Royal Family and handle threats to British security. But it was true. He really *was* a Royal Rabbit.

Shylo briefly thought of his brother, Maximilian, and his five other siblings who had always cruelly teased him. He was sure things would be different on his return home. He wouldn't let them bully him any more, not now he was a brave Knight of the Crown!

A moment later, his bedroom door opened and Belle de Paw appeared in a pink nightdress decorated with shiny silver sequins. Her soft amber fur was standing on end because she had just got out of bed. Unlike little Shylo, she was rubbing her eyes and yawning sleepily. '*Oh là là,*' she murred in her soft French accent, realizing why Shylo was bouncing on the bed. 'You're leaving The Grand Burrow today.'

Shylo stopped bouncing and hopped lightly on to the floor. 'I can almost smell the sweet scents of the forest,' he told her happily, pressing a paw to his chest where his heart was swelling with longing. 'Harvest will be finished and the fields will be full of spilled grain and discarded corn for us to collect. Mother makes the very best corn and barley stew.'

Belle de Paw smiled at the little bunny, of whom she had grown so fond, and reached out to straighten the red eyepatch he wore to cure his squint. 'We will miss you,' she murred, patting him gently. 'You have not been with the Royal Rabbits for long, but you are one of us now. And, don't tell the others, but in my opinion you are the *cleverest* of the team!'

'We've had lots of adventures together, haven't we?' Shylo said proudly, recalling the time they had sneaked into the Queen's private apartments to return the precious Siberian Diamond and nearly been eaten by corgis. Who'd have imagined that a simple country rabbit would have an adventure like that?

'And we will have many more when you come back to us. But remember, you must keep our organization secret,' she warned him gravely. 'No one must know.'

'What will I tell my family?' asked Shylo.

His mother was aware that he was a Royal Rabbit because he'd sent her the medal he'd earned for his first mission and Shylo's old friend Horatio had then told her the truth about Shylo's whereabouts. Horatio had stressed that she must keep all that a secret. But now Shylo wondered where the rest of his family thought he was. How was he going to explain his absence to them?

Belle picked up his paw and turned it over to reveal the Badge, the red palm that was the special mark of a Royal Rabbit. 'Hmmmm,' she murred thoughtfully, then her brown eyes lit up with an idea. 'You will tell them that you work on a beetroot farm. That is why your paw is red.'

Shylo grinned and gazed at her with affection. 'I think *you're* the cleverest of the team,' he said.

'That is why you are so dear to me, Shylo!' she laughed. 'Because you never doubt me. Now hurry and get dressed so you can make the journey home!'

After dressing and feasting on a carrot and celery smoothie sprinkled with watercress, and a large slice of lettuce with honey, Shylo hopped off down the winding corridors of The Grand Burrow to the war room for the usual morning meeting with Nelson, the Generalissimo. As he reached the big double doors, Frisby, the plump, white rabbit whose ceremonial red-and-gold uniform stretched over her round belly and who flaunted her title of 'Major-domo' as if she was the most important rabbit in The Grand Burrow, barred his way with her bejewelled gold staff.

'There's something very odd going on in there!' she whispered to Shylo, twitching her nose and narrowing her eyes. 'Very odd indeed. I'd come back later if I were you.'

'I'm sure I can handle it,' Shylo declared, putting on an important voice. He might not have been as strong as the four very high ranking Hopster rabbits,

Clooney, Zeno, Laser and Belle de Paw, but he was still a Royal Rabbit and always tried to act like a Hopster even when he didn't really feel like one. 'Now please let me in or I'll be late for the meeting!'

Frisby clicked her tongue and huffed. 'Don't say I didn't warn you.' Reluctantly, she opened the door and announced the little bunny.

Shylo was surprised to see that the Generalissimo was not at his desk or leaning over the map table. He was on the floor on all four paws with his tail in the air and the Hopster rabbits around him didn't seem worried that their elderly leader was in such an undignified position. In fact, besides Laser, the straight-talking American doe, who was standing over the Generalissimo, giving instructions of some kind, none of them even seemed to have noticed.

Clooney, the dapper and handsome buck, was lounging on the sofa in his immaculately pressed black tuxedo, crisp white shirt and scarlet bow tie, stroking his whiskers. Belle de Paw, who was usually at the periscopes, looking into the rooms of Buckingham Palace above them, was arranging the feather fascinator on her head in front of the large gilt mirror. Studying the map table was Zeno, the enormous black and muscly Marshal of the Thumpers, the highly trained fighter rabbits. Old Horatio, Nelson's battle-ravaged brother, missing most of his left ear and sporting a long scar down one cheek, was sitting in an armchair with the stump of his lost hind paw resting on a stool, reading a book.

'Push your heels towards the ground, Generalissimo,' said Laser, putting her paws on her hips and tapping the whip in her belt. The red, white and blue fur on her arms, dyed in the stars and stripes of the American flag, shone brightly in the lamplight.

Shylo hopped over. 'May I ask what you're doing?' he

murred softly, assuming that if none of the Hopsters thought it peculiar then neither should he. Frisby was clearly overreacting.

'Humans call it yoga,' said Laser in her American drawl. 'But I like to call it Bendy Bunnies.' She grinned at Shylo, revealing a gold tooth. 'The Generalissimo has a bad back. He's getting older and—'

'Steady!' growled Nelson.

'Sorry, Generalissimo, but Royal Rabbits gotta stay healthy.'

Nelson pushed himself up with a great deal of huffing and puffing. Laser handed him his walking stick and he took a moment to steady himself – standing with your head upside down can make you very dizzy. 'If I remember rightly, today is the day you're heading home for a week's leave.' He looked down at Shylo with his kind old eyes. 'Now I need to tell you three important things before you go.'

Shylo gazed up at him, one ear flopping over his eyepatch because Nelson's face was very serious and, when Nelson got serious, Shylo got a little nervous. After all, the Royal Rabbits are a secret order dedicated to fighting evil across the world - so Shylo guessed he was about to face some kind of challenge, like duelling with the foul Ratzis, defeating the Russian minks, meeting the foxes in the Fox Club or heading off to Hampstead to find a white tiger. His stomach made a funny gurgling noise. Definitely not hunger this time.

'One: don't forget who you are. You're a Royal Rabbit who has earned his place among our secret order. Two: you are braver than you know. Three: don't get too comfortable up there in the countryside. We want you back in seven days' time to help watch over the King and Queen of Holland's state visit next week.'

'And four,' added Horatio, hobbling across the room

on his walking stick, 'life is an adventure. Anything in the world is possible - by will and by luck, with a moist carrot, a wet nose and a slice of mad courage!' He pulled the little bunkin into his arms and a lump formed in Shylo's throat because, as happy as he was to be going home, he was sad to be leaving too.

## CHAPTER TWO

S hylo set off on the underground Rabbit Rail deep beneath Green Park, accompanied by Laser, Zeno, Belle de Paw and Clooney, who all had a meeting at the Fox Club under the Prime Minister's residence at Number Ten Downing Street. They had insisted on first seeing Shylo safely into the van that came to London once a week to deliver vegetables to a posh hotel. While Shylo hitched a ride back to the countryside in the van, the Hopsters would take the Rabbit Rail to the Fox Club for their meeting.

Long ago, the Royal Rabbits had taken great trouble to build a complex network of tunnels underground to enable them to move swiftly and efficiently around London without being seen. Now, as he whizzed along with his ears flapping in the wind, Shylo thought how funny it was that all the people above, walking to work or cycling under the trees, had no idea what was below their feet.

Shylo felt proud to be with these Hopster rabbits. To be *one of them*. He might not have the confidence of Clooney or the strength of Zeno, the wit of Laser or the cunning of Belle de Paw, but as Horatio had said to him when he first left the warren: '*I have great faith in you ... You're going to discover that there's more to you than you ever imagined.*' And now Shylo knew that his old friend had been right. He had come all the way from the countryside to London, on his own, and helped the Royal Rabbits solve many plots and defeat the evil Ratzis.

He lifted his chin and smiled happily at the thought of seeing his mother again and making her proud, even though he knew he could never tell the rest of his family the truth about his adventures in The Grand Burrow.

Once the train stopped at the Weeping Willow, Shylo followed the other rabbits along a tunnel that led to the city above. He could feel his heart jumping about in his chest like a cricket. He wasn't fond of the human world. It was full of dogs and cats and - in the countryside - people with guns, like Farmer Ploughman who had shot and killed Shylo's father when the bunkin was a kitten. No, he did not like the human world at all.

The group stopped beneath a big, round metal object with small holes in it that allowed light to stream in. Zeno, being the strongest, pushed it up far enough to see out. The rumbling noise of cars and buses grew louder.

Shylo squeezed in beside the Marshal of the Thumpers and looked out. He could see the pavement, bollards, parked cars and a few human feet shuffling hurriedly past.

They both dropped back down into the tunnel.

'We're close to the hotel where Shylo will get the van that'll take him home,' said Zeno as quietly as he could, which wasn't very quietly at all because of his booming voice. 'But we need to get round the back where they take deliveries. Once the coast is clear, I'll hold this open and we'll shoot across to the alleyway opposite and hide behind the bins. Got it?'

Belle de Paw, Laser and Clooney nodded. 'Got it,' they replied in unison.

Shylo just nodded. He was unable to speak because his chin was wobbling and his teeth were chattering.

Why was he so nervous? His stomach made a whining noise, as if he'd swallowed a kitten who was very unhappy to find itself in his belly.

'Don't worry, bunkin,' whispered Laser kindly. 'You're only nervous because you care. It means a lot to you to be going home.'

'You'll get home safely, Shylo,' murred Belle de Paw softly.

'And, if you don't, we'll remember what a delightful little rabbit you were,' murred Clooney, grinning.

'That's not funny,' Laser snapped.

'Be quiet, you two. We're on an important mission,' said Belle de Paw bossily.

Zeno lifted the round lid again and looked up and down the street.

'Go!' he growled suddenly, raising it higher to let them through.

One by one, the rabbits darted out into the glare of

day and the noisy chaos of the human world.

Shylo scampered after the bigger rabbits, almost tripping over his clumsy hind paws. He didn't dare look about him in case he saw something scary, like a dog, or a rat, or a human. He dodged a bollard, leaped over a takeaway coffee cup and dashed into the mouth of the alley where the others were hiding behind a row of big, square bins lined up against the wall.

'Good job,' said Laser as Shylo joined them. The small rabbit was panting and shaking, but trying very hard to conceal both.

Zeno lifted his paw and beckoned them on down the alley, over the cobbled stones, towards the courtyard at the other end. He stopped and pressed himself flat against the bricks.

Shylo cowered against the wall. His nose had picked up the scent of dog and he shuddered.

Suddenly, their attention was seized by a rustling

sound in the bins. They turned and froze. Zeno snarled and the fur on his arms bristled. Laser put a paw on her whip and Clooney narrowed his eyes. Belle de Paw bared her claws, preparing to fight. Shylo gulped and his stomach gave that gurgle again. He put a paw there to silence it as his highly sensitive nose picked up a faint whiff of fox.

A bottle dropped on to the ground with a clatter and rolled noisily over the cobbles. A squirrel scampered out of the bin and disappeared down the alley. The rabbits let out a sigh of relief and turned their attention to the courtyard once more.

A white van with the word PLOUGHMAN'S written in big green writing was parked at the back of the hotel. The rear doors were open and Farmer Ploughman was unloading crates of vegetables and carrying them into the building. Shylo recognized him at once. The very same man who had shot his father. The man who had unknowingly driven him up to London in the spring in his crates of cabbages. Shylo remembered the taste of sweet cabbage and his mouth watered.

'Well, Shylo my friend,' Zeno boomed. 'This is where we part ways.' He patted the little rabbit so hard on the back that Shylo nearly choked up his breakfast (which would have been a shame as he'd really enjoyed it).

'Don't get too comfortable and decide not to come back,' said Laser.

'You're one of us,' added Belle de Paw.

'Well, a *smaller* version of us,' quipped Clooney. Laser snarled at him again and he shrugged sheepishly.

Shylo was about to scamper over to the van when a great big Rottweiler wandered out of the hotel and lay down right beside it. The rabbits looked at one another in dismay. How was Shylo going to get to the van now?

Shylo's ears flopped over his face with disappointment. He bit his bottom lip to stop it wobbling, but it wobbled all the same. He watched helplessly as Farmer Ploughman appeared, slammed the van doors shut and walked round to sit behind the wheel. Still the enormous dog didn't move.

'Well, I suppose we could try again next week and bring a juicy bone,' said Clooney with a sympathetic smile, but no one smiled back. Shylo couldn't go home next week because of the Dutch state visit.

Shylo sniffed and hoped that Belle de Paw wasn't going to be sweet to him because then he really would cry, and he was sure Royal Rabbits were much too brave to do that.

Then they heard a whistle. The sort of whistle that demanded attention. It came from above. They raised their eyes to the roof of the hotel.

There, grinning down at them, was a sleek fox.

The fox Shylo had smelled earlier! She was wearing a dashing red tracksuit with a bold white stripe down each leg and reclining on the slope of the roof as if she wanted to soak up a little sun. 'I've got an idea,' she said casually, gazing down at them with her beautiful, intelligent eyes. 'A rabbit like Shylo shouldn't be roughing it in the back of a van anyway.'

Shylo's heart gave a little jump as it was injected with hope, for Red Velvet was a secret agent from the Fox Club at Number Ten Downing Street.

The vixen slid effortlessly down the drainpipe, as if she were a squirrel, not a fox. She looked down at the young bunkin and took his chin in her paw. 'You want to go home, Shylo?'

He nodded.

'Then come with me.'

## CHAPTER THREE

'I wouldn't do this for anyone else,' said Sharp-Tooth-Bushy-Tail, the magnificently glossy and debonair fox also known as ST-BT, who was astride a gleaming motorbike in a secret alleyway near Number Ten Downing Street where Red Velvet had arranged for them to meet, and where the Hopster Rabbits had left them in order to make their meeting on time. 'But I like you, Shylo, and I'm well acquainted with the Warren.'

He grinned at the little rabbit and his pearly white

teeth shone brightly. Then the fox added, with a glint in his eye and a gleam on his tooth, 'There's a vixen near your home who makes a mean Butterscotch on the Rocks, just the way I like it.' He smoothed his lustrous red fur with a paw that sported a large silver ring. 'Luckily for you, I'm not just the most foxifluous fox in the country, I'm also the fastest. Climb up behind me and I'll show you.'

He lowered a helmet over his head then tossed one to Shylo. 'This might be a bit big for you, but it'll hide your rabbit face from humans.'

Shylo caught the helmet, then nearly dropped it because it was heavier than it looked. He had been watching ST-BT with more than a little dread. Was he really going to take him to Northamptonshire on the back of a Harley-Davidson motorbike?

ST-BT and his network of urban foxes, known as the Backstreet Brushes, looked after the Prime Minister

(ST-BT claimed that without him keeping watch the country would go to ruin) and Shylo had seen an enormous portrait of ST-BT riding his motorbike on the wall of the Fox Club under Number Ten Downing Street, but he had never seen the motorbike for real. Now he was being asked to climb on it and sit behind the fox as they sped to the countryside. If he didn't long to see his mother so much, he would have refused. But Red Velvet had explained to ST-BT that this was the only week Shylo was able to go home because Nelson needed him back in seven days and ST-BT had kindly agreed to take him. Although Shylo was almost certain the offer had as much to do with ST-BT wanting to show off his enormous shiny motorbike as wanting to help Shylo get home.

He swallowed his fear and with a big leap he jumped up on to the leather seat behind the fox.

'Hold on tight, little rabbit,' said ST-BT as Shylo

grabbed the fox's white leather jacket.

There was a sudden roar and the bike vibrated beneath Shylo like a terrifying monster, making his teeth chatter and his fur stand on end. Then came a few loud bangs and they were off, zooming down the streets of London and out into the open countryside. And, because they were going so fast, none of the humans, busily talking on their smartphones or in passenger seats, watching movies on their iPads, noticed the fox and the rabbit roaring past them. And, if they did, they simply thought they were two (very small!) people on their way to a fancy-dress party.

As they drove, Shylo found that he was actually beginning to enjoy himself. It was a thrilling sensation riding a motorbike with the most powerful fox in the country. *Goodness*, he thought, *if my brothers and sisters could see me now, they'd be totally AMAZED!* Shylo's ears flew out behind him and he relaxed as

ST-BT glided through the cars and lorries as if he were a bird on the wind.

After a while, they left the motorway and set off down the country lanes. Shylo didn't know where he was exactly, but he could tell he was getting closer to home because he recognized the yellow fields and the hedgerows bursting with blackberries. It smelled familiar too: of the sweet scent of cut wheat and barley and the rich fragrance of the mossy forest. His heart expanded with happiness. It wouldn't be long before he'd see the Warren again.

ST-BT pulled into a farm entrance and drove half a mile up a dirt track to hide beside a small copse at the edge of a field. He switched off the engine and took off his helmet and shook out his luxurious fur. 'Time for a break. You hungry, bunkin?'

'I'm always hungry,' Shylo replied, although, to be honest, he had been so busy enjoying the ride and dreaming of home that he hadn't thought about his stomach. Now it gave a growl, demanding to be fed.

ST-BT pulled out a couple of snack bars from his pocket. 'Ferret and frog flapjack or mouse and mole meringue? Both very tasty in my opinion. In fact, I'd find it hard to choose.' He pretended to weigh them in both paws. 'Ferret - frog - mouse - mole, yes, very difficult. They're *de-lish*!'

'No ... no, thank you,' said Shylo, trying to be polite. 'If you don't mind, I'll nibble a bit of grass and there'll be some spilled wheat in that field, I'll bet.' He climbed down and stretched. He was a bit stiff after sitting in the same position for such a long time. While ST-BT chewed on the mouse and mole meringue, Shylo hopped into the field in search of grain. It wouldn't entirely satisfy him, but it would do until he got home to his mother's corn and barley stew. Oh, the thought of that made his belly ache with longing.

Just then, he was alerted to the sound of a motor and the yelping of dogs.

ST-BT heard it too. His whole body stiffened, his ears pricked and his sharp eyes narrowed. 'A farmer with hunting dogs,' he said. Shylo felt as if a cold wind had just rippled through his fur. He knew all about farmers with guns and packs of dogs. (The Queen's corgis at the palace were very scary, but country dogs were even worse!)

'It appears those dogs have picked up the smell of fox,' growled ST-BT, scratching his chin.

Shylo stood on his hind legs and looked about him. He could just make out a quad bike on the horizon, slowly getting bigger and bigger. Was it coming towards *them*? 'Where's the poor fox?' he asked.

'That would be me,' said ST-BT, pointing at himself in a much too casual way for a fox who was about to be chased by a farmer with a gun and dogs.

Shylo stared at him in alarm.

'They must have picked up our scent somewhere down the lane. Come on, we need to lose them,' ST-BT said, putting his helmet back on.

'And if we don't?' Shylo asked, jumping on to the back of the motorbike as fast as he could and fastening his own helmet before grabbing hold of ST-BT's leather jacket.

'We'll be torn to shreds in the jaws of those dogs.'

The noise of the dogs got louder. The thunder of the quad bike made the ground shake. ST-BT turned on the ignition and the Harley-Davidson sped off with a bang.

Shylo was so close to home. He could almost smell his mother's cooking. How awful would it be if he was eaten by dogs just before he got there!

ST-BT drove skilfully down the farm track and back

out into the lane. He knew it was unlikely that the quad bike would chase them in the road because it was much too dangerous with cars coming and going. But ST-BT enjoyed a bit of danger. Sometimes, in London, life got a little dull. With a wild laugh, he skidded round a corner and drove through a gap in the hedge, into another field of stubble.

Shylo didn't know what the fox was doing, and he was much too scared to ask. He could hear the quad bike and the dogs getting louder. The farmer must think they were poachers, he reasoned - no one would imagine they were a rabbit and a fox on a motorbike! But at least that meant the farmer wouldn't shoot at them.

As they bumped across the field, Shylo managed to glance behind him. To his surprise and horror, he saw that it was *Farmer Ploughman's wife* on the quad bike. Mrs Ploughman's face was red and furious. Two big dogs sat alongside her on the bike, sniffing the air, salivating at the thought of fox and rabbit for dinner, no doubt. Shylo hadn't realized he was already on the Ploughmans' land. The farm must be a lot bigger than he'd thought.

Shylo turned away and squeezed his eyes shut. *Please, please*, he prayed silently to the Great Rabbit in the sky. *Don't let them catch us!*

The Harley-Davidson bucked and bounced and ST-BT made it go faster and faster as if he was relishing the challenge. Shylo buried his face in ST-BT's jacket.

When the ride felt smooth again, Shylo guessed they must be out of the field and back in the lane. He risked peeping with his one eye (remember, the other was hidden behind his red patch) and saw that they were approaching a pub. The sign outside read, THE FOX AND HOUNDS.

*Surely, we're not going in there?* Shylo thought

anxiously, imagining it full of Farmer Ploughmans and hungry hounds with sharp teeth. What he didn't realize was that they were going somewhere FAR WORSE!

ST-BT sped round the pub and into the car park behind at top speed. There, half hidden in a small grove of leafy trees and bushes, was an old wooden shed. ST-BT pulled a horseshoe hanging on the wall and a big door opened. The bike motored into a chamber and the door shut behind them. The fox picked up a stone from a dusty old box, aimed at a row of tin cans lined up above a door and threw it. It hit the second can from the right with a crack. Immediately, a stream of smoke billowed out of a rusty old exhaust pipe, enveloping them. 'That's to hide the smell of fox,' said ST-BT. 'We should wait here for a while, until the danger has passed.'

A door swung open like a big dark mouth. Shylo was suddenly overcome by the smell of fox. It was musty and strong and caught in the back of his throat, making his eyes water.

'Don't fear, bunkin - you're with me, remember?' said ST-BT.

Shylo gulped. The only other time he had smelled this much fox was at the Fox Club, but there the foxes were friendly and had a special relationship with the Royal Rabbits. His experience of country foxes was not as pleasant ... the foxes near the Warren most certainly ate rabbits, *lots* of rabbits! Outside, he could hear the frantic yelping of dogs as they lost their scent. What choice did Shylo have? Fox or hound?

The smell of fox grew stronger and Shylo heard voices. He was gripped with terror, but his heart told him to trust ST-BT; he just hoped that trust was not misplaced.

ST-BT revved his motorbike and then drove through the smoke, right into the middle of a pub full of foxes. Like the Fox Club, there was a bar with stools, and tables and chairs where foxes sat and drank and played cards. But this place was nothing like as polished and gleaming as the Fox Club. It was rough and dusty, with wooden walls and naked light bulbs hanging from a shabby wooden ceiling. The foxes stopped what they were doing and stared at the incredibly foxifluous ST-BT.

A vixen in white breeches, black boots, a white cravat at her neck and a scarlet jacket done up with gold buttons stepped forward. 'Well, if it isn't my old friend ST-BT,' she said with a wide smile. 'I'll bet you're as thirsty as a dashing red fox who's just motored up from London on a Harley-Davidson.' She handed him a cocktail and ran her eyes over Shylo. 'Did you bring your own dinner?'

Shylo realized that he was now being watched by *all* the foxes in the pub. He tried to make himself smaller, drawing his head into his shoulders.

One fox put out his paw. It was so close, Shylo could almost feel the claws against his fur.

With a swift movement, and without spilling a single drop of his cocktail, ST-BT grabbed the paw. 'No you don't,' he said coolly. His voice was deep and masterful and it stilled every fox in the room. 'This is Shylo Tawny-Tail,' he growled. 'And he's with me.'

Shylo peered around sheepishly. The vixen smiled at him without allowing the surprise to show on her face.

'Welcome to the Fox & Fox, Shylo,' she said. 'I'm Riot. What can I get you?'

## CHAPTER FOUR

A s much as Shylo trusted ST-BT's ability to keep the other foxes under control, he wasn't going to take any chances. One snap of a jaw or swipe of a paw and it would all be over before ST-BT could say, 'Didn't I just tell you he's with me?' So Shylo followed ST-BT to a table and made sure he sat right beside him. After all, they were probably going to be here for some time, until the danger of Farmer Ploughman's wife and the dogs had passed.

Riot handed him a glass of juice. It was purply-pink

in colour. He didn't want to be rude and smell it (his mother had brought him up to be a well-mannered bunny) so he took a small sip. *Hmmmm*, he'd never tasted anything like it before. It wasn't unpleasant, but it had a rather sour aftertaste. Shylo frowned. He was surprised he didn't recognize the vegetable - Shylo had tasted every vegetable, even Brussels sprouts, which most young rabbits found disgusting!

'What is it?' he asked.

'The speciality of the house,' Riot replied proudly. 'Ferret blood with bat spit.'

Shylo went green, then pink and finally turned grey. His stomach gave a groan and he thought he was going to be sick.

ST-BT laughed and patted him on the head. 'Country foxes are a little unsophisticated,' he whispered. 'Here, try this.' He passed Shylo his Butterscotch on the Rocks. Shylo took a gulp and the effect was instant.

It was sweet and rich and creamy and his stomach stopped churning. He shivered, relieved not to have vomited in front of all the foxes.

One ear flopped over his eyepatch as he sank back into his chair. He still felt a little sick. Really, he just wanted to get home to his mother. This place made him feel less like a Royal Rabbit and more like the weak and feeble bunkin he'd been in his previous life. He remembered what Horatio had told him when he'd set off into the unknown that first time, all those months ago, that life was an adventure, that anything was possible, *by will and by luck, with a moist carrot, a wet nose and a slice of mad courage*, and Shylo felt a little of his confidence return.

ST-BT spent time talking to the other foxes. He wasn't in any rush. He was enjoying his drink and was interested to hear how things were in the countryside. Life was considerably better since fox-hunting had been outlawed, but farmers still laid traps, shot at the foxes with their guns and got angry when they killed hens and stole their eggs. ST-BT reasoned that there were so many hens, what was one or two less?

Shylo sat patiently and listened, but he wished ST-BT would finish his drink so he could go home. Soon he began to twitch and squirm, fidget and jiggle. At last, ST-BT drained his glass and stood up.

'It's been interesting talking to you all,' he said, climbing on to his Harley-Davidson and winking at Riot, who fluttered her eyelashes at him and smiled. 'But it's time I got back to Number Ten. It's not wise to leave the Prime Minister alone for too long!'

Shylo jumped on behind him and was relieved when the big door opened to allow them to leave. He felt even better out in the fresh country air and drew big gulps into his lungs, dispelling the smell of fox. As they motored round to the front of the pub, he saw Mrs Ploughman's quad bike parked outside. He couldn't help but smile at the thought of the angry farmer's wife having a drink in there while *he* and ST-BT had been right below her, having one too.

It wasn't long before Shylo began to pick up the scent of home. He recognized the big, green, leafy forest where he had grown up. His heart gave a jump and his ears stood to attention, and he suddenly felt full of energy and excitement.

ST-BT stopped the motorbike. 'I think it's best I leave you here, Shylo.' He grinned, baring his teeth that were long and sharp like daggers. 'I'm not sure you'd be able to explain how you came to be riding a Harley-Davidson with a fox to the rest of your Warren. Some things are best kept secret.'

Shylo hopped to the ground. It was good to feel the

earth beneath his paws. 'Thank you, ST-BT,' he murred.

'You take care, little rabbit,' he said, most foxifluously. 'And remember - any trouble with the local foxes and you just say you're a friend of mine. Understood?'

'Understood,' Shylo replied. The motorbike let out a loud bang then disappeared up the lane, leaving Shylo alone but happy. He was finally going to see his family.

With his heart as warm and fluffy as a freshly baked bun, he hurried towards his home. He kept vigilant, for the countryside was full of danger. Birds of prey circled in the sky and foxes prowled in the long grasses, and, even though ST-BT had told him to mention his name, Shylo was wise enough to know that he'd have little time for that if he was about to be eaten.

At last, he reached the Warren, where his community

of rabbits lived in a cluster of burrows at the edge of the forest. It was mid-morning and all was quiet. He wondered where everyone was. Even though most rabbits would be in the fields, gathering food or in their homes underground, there was always someone about. Today, however, there was no one.

The sight of the Burrow caused a lump to form in Shylo's throat. How often had he sat beneath the Weeping Willow in Green Park and dreamed of this very spot? Although he had never really fitted in and his siblings had teased him and made him feel small, this was home. It was where he had grown up, before he'd found a place among the Royal Rabbits and started a new life of adventure. He couldn't wait to surprise his mother.

He hopped into the mouth of the tunnel and scampered down into the soft dampness that was so familiar to him. It smelled of sweet earth and rabbit, as it always had. He reached the kitchen, expecting to see his mother at the stove, cooking lunch, but it was empty. He could tell that his family had been here that morning because their breakfast bowls were still on the table. Seven places laid: one for Mother, three down each side for his three brothers and three sisters ... except now he looked, there were *eight* places laid. There was another bowl at the end, which hadn't been touched. Who was that for? His excitement faded. Who was this mysterious rabbit that had taken his place?

He was probably big and strong and athletic like Maximilian, or perhaps it was a doe who was fleet of foot and elegant like Elvira. Maybe his mother had grown to love this rabbit more than him. After all, Shylo was the runt of the litter, the weakest and feeblest of her kittens. She couldn't know how much being a Royal Rabbit had changed him. Perhaps he'd been foolish to come home. He hadn't fitted in before so why did he think he would now? He should return to The Grand Burrow where he belonged and where he was loved.

With a heavy heart, Shylo left.

He would wait at Horatio's burrow until Farmer Ploughman's van went to London again the following week. No one would know he'd ever been here.

Dragging his paws, he began to shuffle through the forest. Just as he was about to leave the Warren, he heard a voice he recognized. His breath caught in his throat, his ears pricked and he turned round in surprise. 'Mother?'

'Shylo!' she murred, staring at him with eyes as round as moons. 'Is that really you?'

'It really is me!' he replied and the sight of her standing there, looking uncertain, made his heart leap and all his doubt evaporate like mist in sunshine.

She opened her arms and Shylo fell into them, smelling everything he loved about home.

'Oh, I've missed you,' she sighed, closing her eyes and pressing her face against his. 'I've missed you so much.'

Shylo wasn't going to mention the eighth place at the table - he didn't want to spoil the moment - but then he couldn't help himself. He *had* to know. 'Mother, who's the new rabbit who's come to stay?'

'What new rabbit?' she asked.

'The one you've laid a place for at the end of the table.'

Mrs Tawny-Tail cupped Shylo's face in her paws and gazed at him with tenderness. 'That, my darling, is for *you.*'

'For *me?*' he gasped.

'For you.' She sighed and her eyes shone with tears. 'Every day I hoped you'd come home. So I laid a place

for you, just in case.'

Shylo danced for joy round his mother. 'Everything's just as I imagined it would be!' he sang happily. 'It's perfect!'

But his mother's smile didn't reach her eyes and Shylo stopped dancing, sensing her worry. 'Isn't it?' he asked, feeling his ears droop.

'I'm afraid not,' she said. 'The Elders called a meeting in the Hollow. It's just finished. Something strange is going on in the forest. Perhaps it's nothing, but ...' She hesitated. 'Walk with me, Shylo. I think you should see for yourself.'

## CHAPTER FIVE

Shylo and his mother wandered deeper into the forest. A dragonfly with iridescent wings darted through the shafts of light that pierced the leaves above them. Shylo thought how beautiful the forest was. However, it wasn't long before its beauty was ruined by a musty, pungent smell of dirty rabbits. It wasn't unpleasant. In fact, after the strong foxy smells at the Fox & Fox, it was really quite appealing to Shylo! Then he heard the twang of a banjo and a whining voice singing: 'Rabbits, rabbits, follow me, follow me . . .' Then many other voices joined in tunelessly.

'What *is* that?' Shylo asked.

The voices grew louder and he began to notice clothes hanging on bushes and empty sacks of grain discarded among bottles of apple juice and rotting vegetables. Wasps buzzed about the rubbish and Shylo edged away. He had once been stung on the nose by a wasp, and it had grown so red and swollen that it had looked as if his snout had sprouted a tomato. He was keen to avoid that happening again!

'You've seen enough. Come,' said his mother, turning round, not wanting Shylo to get too close. But the little rabbit was curious. He crept nearer to where the music was coming from. 'Shylo!' his mother insisted, but it was too late.

'Hi, Mama, join us!' came a voice as soft and silky as a breeze. Mrs Tawny-Tail froze, but Shylo stepped out of the trees, into the clearing. The voice belonged to a small pale ginger rabbit who was sitting on a simple chair in the middle of a throng of rabbits, playing the banjo. The rabbit was wearing a multicoloured patchwork coat that reached to the ground. His fur was shaggy, like a lion's mane, and tied into a bun on the top of his head in a style rabbits call a 'bun-bun'. Unlike the rabbits Shylo was familiar with, this rabbit had floppy ears that hung down either side of his face, decorated with lots of metal earrings. He had large amber-coloured eyes and a small mouth, and when he smiled Shylo saw that some of his teeth were gold and that he was also missing one of the front two.

'Thank you,' said Shylo's mother tightly, stepping up beside her son. 'But we should be getting home.'

Shylo saw that Maximilian and Elvira were among the group of rabbits who crowded round the ginger rabbit. Although they looked astonished to see *him*, it quickly became obvious that they did not want him and their mother to spot *them*. They shuffled to hide behind the other rabbits and Shylo pretended he hadn't noticed them and looked away.

'Hey, bro,' said the ginger rabbit in a strong American accent, looking directly at Shylo. 'Come join us. Everyone's welcome here.'

A wiry little weasel stood up and puffed out his chest with self-importance. 'This is Harlequin,' he said in a nasal voice. 'The greatest rabbit in the world. A Magic Rabbit with unparalleled powers. When *he* invites you to join him, you do not turn round and hurry home.' All the rabbits nodded in agreement.

'Well ...' Shylo began, curious to know why Harlequin was the greatest rabbit in the world and what his brother and sister were doing here with him. He wondered whether being a magic rabbit meant he was some sort of magician.

'No, thank you,' said Shylo's mother firmly. 'We

really must be getting home.'

'Another time then, Mama?' purred Harlequin. 'We're not going anywhere.'

'No, we're not,' agreed the weasel. 'This is our home now.'

Shylo and his mother walked off into the forest and the music started up again, floating on the breeze in a hypnotic chant.

'There's something very worrying about Harlequin and his band of followers,' said Mrs Tawny-Tail, who rarely said a bad word about anyone, not even tiresome, ill-mannered rabbits. 'And I'm not just talking about the piercings and the smell of unwashed bodies. They're very lazy and don't want to work, which is why young rabbits who know no better join them. They laze about all day, listening to Harlequin play the banjo, just taking what they need.'

'Have they built a warren?'

'Oh, no, they're much too lazy for that. And the Elders say they've been stealing from our stores of grain and corn which we need for the winter months. It's all very well doing nothing all summer, but when winter comes, and they have no proper homes to stay warm in and no supplies to eat, they'll find themselves in trouble. If they steal all our supplies, we'll be in trouble too.'

'Perhaps they'll move on when the cold weather sets in?' Shylo suggested hopefully.

'I'm afraid the Elders think they're here to stay,' said Mrs Tawny-Tail anxiously. 'The trouble is Maximilian and Elvira have joined them. You saw how they hid a moment ago? They think I don't know, but I do.' She frowned. 'I'm worried because ...' She hesitated.

'Because?' Shylo asked, feeling a niggle wiggling its way into his stomach like a worm into an apple. That niggle usually meant something wasn't right (but it could also mean he was hungry). Horatio had told him to always listen to his niggles, hunger ones or otherwise, because you never knew.

Mrs Tawny-Tail sighed heavily. 'Maximilian believes everything Harlequin tells him, and will do whatever Harlequin wants him to do. I'm afraid Harlequin is a bad influence and encourages Maximilian to steal things too. He seems to have a charisma that some rabbits find hard to resist. As for Elvira, she just does whatever Maximilian does.'

Shylo shook his head. 'I'm sure Maximilian and Elvira will soon get bored and come home.'

'The Elders have forbidden any rabbit from the Warren to go near him, but Maximilian and Elvira are there all the time. They're not afraid of anyone. At least my other kittens have respect for the Elders.' Mrs Tawny-Tail smiled. 'But you're back!' she exclaimed happily, trying to forget her worries. 'A Royal Rabbit no less. I'm so proud of you, Shylo.'

'You're the only one who knows,' he whispered, growing taller in the beam of her admiration. Of all the rabbits in the world, it was his mother he wanted to impress the most.

'I keep the medal you sent me in a special drawer in my bedroom. I treasure it. I always believed in you, Shylo. I'm pleased that *you* finally learned to believe in yourself.'

Shylo put his paw in hers and they hopped home together.

# CHAPTER SIX

It was lunchtime when Shylo's siblings, Wilton, Willow, Erica and Lewie, arrived home to find their brother in the kitchen and, without Maximilian there to encourage them to tease Shylo, they threw their arms round their little brother and told him how much they'd missed him - which they secretly had, quite a lot.

'Mother told us you went to make your own way in the world!' said Erica. 'Where did you go?'

'Have you been on an adventure?' asked Wilton.

'Why did you stay away so long?' enquired Willow.

Lewie looked a little sheepish and his grey ears drooped anxiously. 'Was it because we were unkind to you?'

Shylo sat down at the table and showed them his red paw. 'I've been working on a beetroot farm,' he explained, remembering what Belle de Paw had told him. The four rabbits peered at it curiously. Shylo continued. 'It's quiet there and the other rabbits are very friendly. But I missed all of you.' And he looked from one to the other and realized that he truly had. 'I had seven days' leave and wanted to surprise you.'

Shylo really was very happy to be home. He ate two whole bowls of corn and barley stew and told his siblings made-up stories about the beetroot farm. He longed to tell them about his *real* adventures with the Royal Rabbits of London. How he'd saved the Queen from *two* plots, foiled the vile Ratzis, escaped from

Rat Central at the very top of the tallest building in London and found the stolen Siberian Diamond, the biggest diamond in the world. How he wished he could tell them *that*.

Shylo was enjoying the warm feeling of belonging when he heard voices coming down the tunnel. It was Maximilian and Elvira. The niggle in Shylo's belly grew stronger. He knew for sure now that it wasn't hunger.

Maximilian hopped into the Burrow and Shylo stared at him in amazement. He hadn't noticed earlier because Maximilian had been further away, but now, up close, his brother looked very different! He had piercings all the way up and down his ears and one big silver ring through his nose. He had shaved his fur very short and was wearing a grubby shirt that Shylo didn't recognize. Elvira had also pierced her ears and had painted an excessive amount of black charcoal round her eyes, which made her look strange. In fact, the two of them looked very peculiar indeed.

*Why, they look just like Harlequin!* Shylo thought. He shuddered as Maximilian approached with his usual swagger, smirk and his air of menace. Some things, it seemed, didn't change.

'Well, well, well, look what the cat dragged in,' he sang. He sauntered over to Shylo, took his red eyepatch in his paw and pulled it hard. Shylo gasped. He stared in horror as Maximilian opened his big mouth and laughed, then let go of the patch and watched it snap back, slapping Shylo painfully on the eye. Shylo yelped. He put a paw over his face and his siblings laughed, just like they always had.

How could a Royal Rabbit of London, a brave Knight of the Crown, a Spy of the Rabbit Rules of Secret Craft, allow this to happen and do *nothing* to stop it? How was it that, after all he'd been through in London, he was unable to stand up for himself here?

His eyes stung with disappointment and frustration that Maximilian still had that kind of power over him.

'Maximilian! Harlequin wouldn't like to see you do that. He's a peace-loving Magic Rabbit. Didn't he say we have to love each other?' said Elvira sharply.

'Oh, yes ... and if we obey him we'll be happy Magic Rabbits,' replied Maximilian a bit sheepishly. He ruffled the fur between Shylo's ears. 'Sorry, bro. I didn't mean to hurt you. It was just a joke.' He laughed again. 'You're meant to laugh too. Where's your sense of humour?'

But Shylo couldn't laugh. He wanted to cry!

'So what happened to you, Shylo? Where did you go?' Elvira asked. Shylo felt very small beside his two big, strong, glossy siblings. He didn't feel like a Royal Rabbit any more; he felt like a coward. It was as if everything he had achieved in London had never happened.

'He's been working on a beetroot farm,' said Wilton. 'Look at his paw. It's red!'

But Elvira and Maximilian weren't interested in Shylo's red paw. In fact, they weren't really interested in him at all. They only wanted to talk about Harlequin.

'Harlequin has the most beautiful voice!' cooed Elvira with admiration when she was sure her mother wasn't listening. Lewie glanced at Wilton and rolled his eyes. They were bored of hearing about Harlequin. But Maximilian was keen to show off to Shylo.

'If you're lucky,' he said, 'Harlequin lets you sit close to him so you can hear him better.'

'Are *you* allowed to sit close to him?' asked Shylo.

'Well ... no,' replied Maximilian, shuffling uncomfortably. 'Not yet. But I will be. I know it. I mean, he's sure to pick me, isn't he? I'm bigger and stronger than the other rabbits, after all.'

'The rabbits in Harlequin's inner circle are called

Golden Rabbits,' Elvira added. 'They're the only rabbits allowed into his tent. They're special. They go on secret missions, but we don't know what those are exactly. They're just secret and, well, special.' She sighed and put a paw over her heart. 'Harlequin says he's going to rule the world and bring back the Great Rabbit Empire and, if we follow him, we'll share his magic, and those who don't will be our slaves!'

Shylo thought that sounded completely ridiculous and was surprised Elvira and Maximilian believed it. 'What kind of magic?' he asked.

'That's secret,' said Maximilian, smirking. 'Sorry, bro. Unless you're in, you're out, and if you're out you can't know any secrets.' He shrugged and hopped into the kitchen. 'What's for lunch, Mother? I'm hungry!'

Shylo turned to Elvira and frowned. 'You don't really believe that rubbish, do you?' he said.

Elvira's face twitched with irritation. 'Harlequin is

going to find the Golden Carrot, Shylo,' she hissed crossly. 'And when he does he's going to be the most powerful rabbit in the whole world!'

Shylo's ears stood to attention. He knew all about the legend of the Golden Carrot from one of the dusty old books he used to read in Horatio's burrow. But before he could ask Elvira for more information she had hopped off to join Maximilian at the table.

Shylo needed to investigate. It was his Royal Rabbit duty! He looked down at the red Badge on his paw and lifted his chin. Maximilian might be strong and athletic, but he wasn't very smart. Shylo was clever - he knew that - and it was the one thing that gave him confidence. He'd get to the bottom of what Harlequin was planning.

Later that afternoon, he managed to get time alone with Maximilian and Elvira. He sidled up to them and whispered, in a soft voice so no one else could hear: 'I'd like to meet Harlequin properly.'

Maximilian smirked. 'Ah, I knew you were interested and I know why! You think that Harlequin can use his magic to stop you being a scrawny, pathetic little disappointment. Well, he can ... if you believe in him. Peasie the weasel was once like you and now he's as brave as a bull, thanks to Harlequin.'

'Harlequin will give you the world if you join him,' added Elvira. 'He invites rabbits from all over the globe to join him. Everyone's welcome. Come with us tomorrow and we'll introduce you. You don't look like much, but Harlequin loves everyone just as they are. He loves us all.' She put a paw on Shylo's shoulder. 'Don't tell Mother we're taking you, though, or you'll get us into trouble.'

That night Shylo's mother made a feast. There were all sorts of delicious things to eat and no one prepared them like Mrs Tawny-Tail: celery and cabbage wraps, carrot and mint dips, pumpkin and sweet potato crispies, all washed down with Root and Ginger Snifter, which was a special drink that Shylo's grandmother created, and only Shylo's mother knew how to make. The food in The Grand Burrow was good, but it was nothing like his mother's. Shylo gobbled it all up with relish, slurped the Snifter greedily and realized how much he'd missed it all.

Word had got out that Shylo had returned and gradually rabbits from all over the Warren came to see him, out of curiosity more than affection. Shylo had always been a loner.

'He's changed,' they whispered to each other.

'He's got an air of adventure about him,' they said.

Shylo knew he had changed too. Feeling like an outsider was normal for the little bunkin, though now he didn't feel different because he was weak and small, but because he'd seen things and had adventures the country rabbits of the Warren could only dream of. His experience of the world had grown and his understanding of rabbit nature had too. He knew he wasn't the same Shylo who had left in the spring. He was happy to be back, but was surprised that his burrow and their little corner of the forest looked smaller to him now.

He thought of his new friends in The Grand Burrow and realized how much he loved being part of their group. How proud he was to be a Royal Rabbit, and how much satisfaction he got from being a valued member of the team.

That night Shylo snuggled up in his old bed and his mother kissed him tenderly as she always used to do before he went to sleep and, for a moment, he felt like a kitten again, safe and secure. He wrapped his arms round her and nuzzled against her; she smelled of home and everything he loved about it. But, once she was gone and he was alone, he felt strange again. It was as if he'd outgrown his old life. He was no longer a kitten, but a grown rabbit still trying to fit into his kitten things.

He closed his eyes, but frightening thoughts invaded his mind. Harlequin was taking over the forest, which was filled with flickering lights, dancing shadows, strange voices and eerie songs as more followers arrived. Rabbits young and old were all chanting, 'The Golden Carrot is coming. It's here! It's time. Feel the magic-ragic.'

When Shylo finally found sleep, it was troubled and fretful.

## CHAPTER SEVEN

The following afternoon, with a very niggly niggle in the pit of his belly, Shylo set off with Maximilian and Elvira to be properly introduced to Harlequin. Birds tweeted in the trees as they settled down to roost and small flies danced and twirled in the rays of golden light that fell through the canopy of leaves above. Shylo felt a little nervous. He'd faced greater challenges than this, like the evil Ratzis. Harlequin wasn't a Ratzi, but there was something very sinister about him that Shylo didn't like.

73

It wasn't long before he once again heard the sound of singing and smelled the ripe and gamey scent of unwashed rabbits. A large gathering came into view through the trees. They were sitting together on the grass in the clearing, their ears rising sharply out of the shadows, swaying to the music and singing. Harlequin was sitting on a tree stump, facing his Magic Rabbits, playing the banjo.

Shylo, Maximilian and Elvira lingered at the back of the crowd until the singing stopped and Harlequin handed his banjo to the weasel.

'Follow me,' said Maximilian importantly and bounded up to Harlequin enthusiastically.

'Hey, Maxi, you've brought a new recruit! You're a good Magic Rabbit. I always reward good Magic Rabbits, don't I?'

Maximilian smiled proudly and puffed out his chest.

Harlequin looked at Shylo with a disinterested air.

Then his amber gaze settled on the red paw and his eyes suddenly narrowed with interest. 'Hey, little rabbit, you were here yesterday, weren't you?' He grinned, revealing his missing tooth. 'Yeah, I recognize a *special* rabbit when I see one. I bet this time you'll wanna stay.' He patted the ground beside him. 'Come sit beside me. Become a Magic Rabbit. Believe in the magic-ragic. Give yourself to me and you'll be free.'

'He gets to sit beside you already?' Maximilian protested jealously. He couldn't understand why Shylo was being so favoured when he'd done nothing to deserve it. Elvira caught her breath and glanced anxiously at Harlequin, waiting for his response.

'We don't raise our voices here, do we, Maxi?' said Harlequin calmly. 'Not if you want to be a *good* Magic Rabbit.'

Maximilian shrank back with a scowl. Shylo thought it odd that Maximilian, who had always been so fearless, was now scared of this small ginger rabbit. He realized then that beneath his boasting Maximilian was just as unsure as the rest of them.

'I said come sit by me,' Harlequin repeated firmly to Shylo, patting the ground beside him a little harder this time. Shylo did as he was instructed - there was something about Harlequin that told him he did not like being disobeyed. 'And, Maxi and Evi, make sure your brother doesn't run off at the end of the ceremony. I wanna talk to him some more. If he becomes a Magic Rabbit, I'll give *him* a special name too.'

Harlequin stood up and hit a large metal gong with a hammer. The rabbits fell silent. Then Peasie the weasel clashed a pair of cymbals and Harlequin addressed the crowd.

'My precious little Magic Rabbits,' he murred in a soft voice as smooth and sweet as toffee. Everyone had to be extremely quiet to hear him. Even the roosting birds seemed to fall silent and listen. 'You have come to me from far and wide. From the hills of the north and the beaches of the south to the plains of the west and the fields of the east, you have travelled far to join my growing community of followers. Why? Because you wanna different life. You want freedom from rules. Freedom from humans who wanna trap you, shoot you, eat you or capture you. I welcome you all. Some of you have left your families to follow me, but you don't need your families because *we* are your family now. Look around you, at the love on your neighbour's face.'

Shylo glanced at Maximilian and saw nothing remotely loving in his expression. His big brother scowled at him as if he wished Shylo would disappear.

'I am your *father*,' Harlequin continued. 'And I will show you, my Magic Rabbits, a better way to live.' He opened his arms wide as if he wanted to embrace them all. There was a ripple of enthusiasm in the crowd. Shylo looked at Maximilian and Elvira, their faces now alight with admiration.

'Feel the magic-ragic.'

A murmur of excitement rippled through the crowd. 'Feel the magic-ragic!' they chanted. Shylo wasn't quite sure what the magic-ragic was. He felt nothing but uneasiness.

'We Magic Rabbits have been searching for something for one thousand years. What is it?' Harlequin continued.

'The Golden Carrot!' they cried.

'Yes, my Magic Rabbits! The Golden Carrot!' There was a cheer from the crowd. Harlequin held up a large yellowed piece of old parchment with both paws. 'I have been studying an ancient map that has been lost for almost two thousand years. I came across it in

America when I was sneaking about in a museum late at night, searching tirelessly for anything that could help me find the Golden Carrot. It's taken me hours of studying to work out exactly where the carrot is buried, but I am in no doubt that this large black cross you see here, which marks the burial site, is beneath the very land we're sitting on. That is why I've led you to this place my Magic Rabbits! The Golden Carrot is HERE! The time is NOW!'

Shylo felt the niggle grow more niggly in his stomach. It was strong and insistent, like a very anxious and agitated worm.

'You will find it for me, my Magic Rabbits. You will dig it up and present it to me. I will use its magical powers to spread *love* throughout the world. To make it a better place. First we take over the farm. Then we take over the country. Finally, we take over the world. We will rebuild the Great Rabbit Empire of the past

80

with the magic of the Golden Carrot and I will be your king. Repeat after me, my Magic Rabbits: Farm, Country, World.'

The rabbits repeated his words: 'Farm, Country, World.'

'Stand and say it again,' he commanded.

The Magic Rabbits stood. Shylo found himself standing too, but he didn't repeat the words.

'Louder. I can't hear you!' said Harlequin.

'FARM! COUNTRY! WORLD!' they cried, in a fever of enthusiasm. The crowd of rabbits began to mob Harlequin and he held up his paws, as if he wanted to bless them all. Shylo had to scamper out of the way to avoid being crushed.

He found Elvira and Maximilian standing a little apart from the frenzy of rabbits. They were talking animatedly to each other.

'This is what we're all waiting for!' Elvira said as

Shylo joined them. 'The Golden Carrot. Magic. Power. Harlequin will rule the Great Rabbit Empire.' Her eyes gleamed as she turned back to Harlequin. 'Isn't he magnificent?'

Harlequin hit the gong again and, as the rabbits sat down obediently, Peasie clashed the cymbals.

'I command you all to dig in every field, ditch and dell. Find the Golden Carrot and bring it to me. The Magic Rabbit who does will be richly rewarded.'

Shylo felt sick. How could Maximilian and Elvira think that taking over the farm was a good thing? Didn't they care about their home? Weren't they worried about what would happen to their family? Did they really believe that this group of unwashed creatures, who called themselves Magic Rabbits, could replace their mother, Erica, Willow, Wilton and Lewie? (He didn't include himself because he knew they'd be only too happy to replace *him*.) He didn't expect them to worry about Harlequin taking over the world like he did because they weren't Royal Rabbits with a duty to fight evil. But he expected them to have more loyalty to their family and the Warren.

Maximilian grabbed Shylo's arm. 'Harlequin specifically asked us to bring you to him and we must do as he said. But don't think you'll be chosen to be a Golden Rabbit. You have to prove your worth before you get that kind of privilege!'

As much as Shylo just wanted to go home and be as far away from this strange group of rabbits as possible, he was also curious to hear what else Harlequin had to say. He'd never seen anyone like him before. So he allowed himself to be pulled along by Maximilian and Elvira into the crowd.

## CHAPTER EIGHT

Suddenly Shylo was once again standing in front of Harlequin. The rabbit's eyes smouldered like molten copper and seemed to burn right through him. Harlequin put an arm round Shylo and drew him away from his siblings and the rest of the throng.

'What a special rabbit you are, Shylo,' said Harlequin in his silky voice, and he looked at the little bunkin with such fondness that Shylo felt a tiny quiver in his heart, at the very core where he felt most unsure.

'When you become a Magic Rabbit, I'll call you Shy.

It suits you, I think. But, besides being a little shy, I see you're also wise and uncommonly intelligent,' Harlequin continued, lowering his voice so no one else could hear what he was saying. 'You're small and weak and uncertain, but I see the real you. The bright and brave rabbit who is full of love. Yes, I can see into your soul and I can see the love there. It burns like a light.'

Shylo's mouth fell open. Could this rabbit truly see into his soul? Perhaps he really was magic. Maybe he could see into the heart of every rabbit and that was why they wanted to follow him.

Harlequin lifted Shylo's paw and ran a surprisingly sharp claw over the red Badge. 'Interesting,' he muttered. There was a strange look on his face. A greedy, menacing look that Shylo didn't like.

He snatched his paw away, but Harlequin smiled knowingly and chuckled. Was it possible that he knew what the Badge meant?

'You're special, Shylo,' Harlequin continued. 'You're not like the others. They're not clever like you. When the Golden Carrot is found, I will restore the Great Rabbit Empire. I'll be king and *you* will be my special advisor. I think you'll be a great help in getting me to the very *heart* of power.'

Shylo saw a glint of evil in his eyes and stiffened. 'Harlequin, where did you find that map?'

A shadow of annoyance darkened the other rabbit's face. 'Do you doubt that it's real?'

'No ... of course not,' Shylo stammered, not liking the cold look in Harlequin's amber eyes which only a moment ago had glowed with warmth.

'I was running away from a security guard in the museum when I accidentally knocked over a piece of wall supposedly from King Arthur's castle at Camelot. When it hit the floor, it shattered into pieces. The map was hidden inside.'

Shylo gasped. His ears stiffened. 'The map was hidden in a piece of King Arthur's wall at Camelot?'

'I knew immediately that it was the real thing - that it would lead me to the Golden Carrot.' He grinned, the gaps in his line of teeth appearing dark and threatening.

Harlequin turned away abruptly to listen to Peasie, who had lifted his ear and was now whispering into it. Shylo noticed how quickly he had turned from affectionate to indifferent and realized how very cunning he was. The little rabbit understood now why rabbits flocked to Harlequin. Like a loving father he offered them a sense of belonging, but it was all nonsense. He didn't love any of them - he just pretended he did. Shylo wondered whether his time with the Royal Rabbits had given him a certain wisdom to see through characters like Harlequin.

But Shylo already had a sense of belonging, didn't

he? He was a Royal Rabbit. He had a group of friends and comrades he knew would stand by him, no matter what. If he didn't have that, would he be seduced by Harlequin like those other rabbits? He didn't think so and he didn't think the Royal Rabbits would fall for Harlequin's fake charm either. They were too intelligent, noble and wise. He wondered why Maximilian and Elvira couldn't see Harlequin for what he was. But then, Shylo had always been the sharpest of the litter.

Maximilian and Elvira rushed over to him.

'Isn't he wonderful?' gushed Elvira.

'Did he say anything to you about the Golden Rabbits?' Maximilian asked anxiously. For the first time, Shylo saw doubt in his brother's eyes.

'No,' Shylo replied. 'He didn't.'

'Good,' said Maximilian with relief. 'I wouldn't want *you* to become one before me.'

'Oh, I wouldn't want to become one before you

either, Maximilian,' said Shylo. Maximilian grinned, pleased. 'I don't want to become a Golden Rabbit *at all*.' Maximilian frowned in surprise. 'Don't you see what's happening here?' Shylo said. 'Don't you care about your family, your home, your Warren?'

'*This* is my home now,' his brother retorted crossly.

'But they don't love you here. Harlequin just *says* he does. He doesn't really think you're special. He doesn't think any of these rabbits are special. He calls you all his Magic Rabbits so you *think* you're special. He's going to use you like slaves to dig up the farm in search of the Golden Carrot so that he can become the most powerful rabbit in the world.'

Maximilian glared at him.

'You don't know what you're talking about,' snapped Elvira. 'Maximilian and I know more about Harlequin than you do.'

'Why don't you go back to that beetroot farm and

you can dye the other paw red?' Maximilian laughed.

'Because you're my brother.' Shylo turned to Elvira and one ear flopped over his eyepatch. 'And you're my sister. And, although I don't like you very much right now, I do love you. You're family. *We're* family, all of us.'

'Oh! Be quiet!' sneered Maximilian. 'Go and give a speech to someone who wants to listen - oh, wait . . . there *isn't* anyone who cares what you think.' He laughed again.

Shylo's bottom lip wobbled and it took a great effort to steady it. Not because he was scared or frightened. Not because he wasn't brave, but because he was hurt. He hoped Maximilian might have missed him during the months he'd been away. He hoped he'd changed, but he hadn't. He was still just as mean as he always had been.

'Look,' Maximilian continued. 'The Golden Carrot

is here, and *I'm* going to find it!'

Shylo knew from his conversation with Harlequin that there was a very strong chance that the Golden Carrot was, indeed, buried here.

He realized he had to stop Harlequin from finding the carrot and taking over the world, and save Maximilian and Elvira from themselves, even though they probably wouldn't thank him for it. Harlequin's followers were now in their thousands and all camping in the forest - *their* forest - and dancing round campfires, singing strange songs. They didn't even seem to worry about predators, or Farmer Ploughman and his shotgun, or his pack of salivating dogs. Perhaps Harlequin was magic after all!

As for the Golden Carrot, that was indeed a concern. If it really *was* buried here on the farm, and Harlequin found it, he would not use its magic to do good, of that Shylo was certain. No, Harlequin would use its magic to give him power, and who knew what kind of malice he would do with it. He recalled Harlequin's chant with growing unease: *Farm, Country, World.* Wasn't it his duty, as a Royal Rabbit of London, to fight evil wherever he found it?

He needed to get a message to The Grand Burrow at once and there was only one way to do that: he had to go to the Fox & Fox.

Shylo shivered. Was he brave enough to go back, on his own?

He lifted his chin and pulled back his shoulders. *I'm a Royal Rabbit,* he reminded himself. *I have to do this so I will. Life is an adventure. Anything in the world is possible - by will and by luck, with a moist carrot, a wet nose and a slice of mad courage!*

He would set off for the Fox & Fox first thing tomorrow.

## CHAPTER NINE

The following morning, the rabbits went off into the fields to gather food as they always did. The harvest was over, but there were parts the machinery had missed and wheat and barley were scattered on the soil. The hedgerows were full of blackberries and elderberries, wild garlic and herbs.

Maximilian and Elvira were heading off again to join Harlequin, even though the Elders had declared it out of bounds for all rabbits of the Warren. Shylo tried to persuade his brother and sister not to go.

'You should come with us, but no, you're too scared to break the rules,' sneered Maximilian. 'You've always been a goody-goody.' He reached for Shylo's eyepatch. As he did so, a paw shot up and grabbed him by the wrist. Maximilian stared at it, then his eyes travelled along the arm until Maximilian saw, to his utter surprise and disbelief, that the paw belonged to Shylo.

'I'm not the same little Shylo that you used to push around,' said Shylo quietly. He stared at his brother's astonished face and didn't so much as blink. 'Don't *ever* snap my patch again.'

Maximilian snatched his paw away, looking shaken. 'Come on, Elvira. Let's go,' he said and, as the two of them disappeared into the bushes, Shylo thought that his brother didn't look quite so big any more.

Shylo felt brave as he hopped across the field towards

the Fox & Fox. It was a golden September morning. Puffs of white cloud moved slowly across a bright blue sky and there were no birds of prey circling above in search of small rabbits like Shylo.

He had stood up to Maximilian at long last. Like all bullies, Maximilian was really a coward underneath, and Shylo was sure that his brother would leave him alone from now on. Standing up to his brother had made Shylo happy. He couldn't have done that a few months ago, before becoming a Royal Rabbit.

He needed to get a message to his friends in The Grand Burrow to warn them about Harlequin and the search for the Golden Carrot. It was his sacred duty to inform them of a potential threat to national security and right now Shylo felt he could do anything, even that. Then he saw the Fox & Hounds pub, and his confidence melted away like ice cream in sunshine.

What if the foxes didn't recognize him? What if he

didn't have time to explain who he was before they fell on him with their sharp teeth and sharp claws? For a moment, he hesitated. Then he thought of the crowds of Magic Rabbits and of Maximilian and Elvira and the danger they could be in ... Maximilian might not be very nice to him, but he was still his brother. Shylo had to find out who Harlequin was, not just because he was a Royal Rabbit but also because he was the only rabbit in the Warren who seemed willing to do something. From what his mother had told him, all the Elders had done was talk. So, refusing to give in to his fears, he hopped over the fields, making sure to keep to the hedges, until he arrived at the little shed at the back of the pub.

Just as ST-BT had done two days earlier, Shylo pulled the horseshoe to open the first set of doors, then he picked a stone from the box and aimed at the row of cans above the inner door. The first stone missed altogether. The second one hit the wrong can. But the third struck the correct one bang in the middle. With a billow of smoke, the door to the Fox & Fox opened and the little bunkin stared, terrified, into the dark throat of the foxes' lair.

For a second, his legs felt so heavy and numb that he wasn't sure he'd be able to move them. Then he gritted his teeth and forced himself forward. But what he didn't see was the broken piece of wood sticking up from the top of the ramp ... Clumsily, his hind paw caught on the wood and he tumbled to the ground, rolling like a barrel right into the middle of the room. Shylo squeezed his eyes shut as the smell of fox enveloped him. His head swam, he saw white teeth, felt sticky wet saliva dropping on to his fur and heard the howling of voices. He curled into a tight ball with his paws about his head to protect it from the jaws that were coming to rip him apart.

But none did.

Tentatively, he opened his eyes. Not one of the foxes looked like they were about to eat him. In fact, they weren't even anywhere near. They were still sitting at their tables, or loitering by the bar, or dealing their cards.

He sat up in bewilderment, blinking away the horrible images conjured up by his overactive mind.

'Hello, little Shylo,' said Riot from behind the bar. 'I didn't expect to see you again!'

The other foxes watched him curiously and a little dismissively, Shylo thought. He was ashamed to admit that he was slightly offended that none of them tried to eat him. He hadn't even needed to mention ST-BT's name. Was it because he was too skinny? He stood up and dusted himself down and acknowledged that there really wasn't very much meat on him. If he were a fox, he wouldn't eat such a scrawny-looking bunny either!

He hopped over to Riot who was pouring a drink. 'I thought they were going to eat me,' he murred.

She grinned, revealing her knife-like eye teeth. 'No, we knew it was you,' she growled softly.

Shylo frowned. 'How?' he asked.

She put her paws on the bar and laughed a deep, throaty laugh. 'How many little bunnies come rolling into the Fox & Fox, do you think?' she chuckled.

'I don't suppose any,' he replied.

'Exactly and, if you don't mind me saying, you're the only rabbit we've ever seen with an eyepatch. We don't get many pirates in here either.' She passed him the drink. 'On the house. Any friend of ST-BT is a friend of mine. Now what can I do for you?'

'I need to get a message to ST-BT,' Shylo murred. 'It's urgently foxifluous!'

Riot nodded. 'I can get it to him by tonight. Don't

you worry. What is it?'

Shylo pulled an envelope out of his jacket pocket. 'I need him to give this letter to Nelson. It's about a rabbit called Harlequin who believes the legendary Golden Carrot is buried right here on the farm.'

'You mean Harlequin the singer and his followers? We've been watching them taking over the forest.' She grinned. 'We've been picking off the odd rabbit, but really it's much too easy. There's no challenge in dopey rabbits wandering about the place in broad daylight. We foxes do like a challenge, you know.'

'Is the Warren more of a challenge for you?' Shylo asked bravely.

'It is, but, like I said, any friend of ST-BT is a friend of mine, so we'll find dinner somewhere else in future.' She tapped the glass with her claw. 'Drink up.'

But Shylo didn't want to and this time he wasn't afraid to say. 'As much as I like you, Riot, this isn't my kind of drink, neither is it a place in which I'd like to linger. So, if you don't mind, I'll hop off home.'

'I don't mind at all,' she said. 'You take care. And, if you don't mind *me* saying, you're a brave bunkin to come in here. The first, actually. Well, the first *live* one.'

## CHAPTER TEN

ST-BT strode along the corridor of The Grand Burrow, towards Nelson's office, with purpose. He cut a dash in his bright scarlet trousers and black boots and it has to be said that he had the most magnificent whiskers of any fox who'd ever lived. He had a very important matter to discuss and there was an air of urgency about the way he marched.

Frisby, the Major-domo, was a little afraid of ST-BT, so she didn't ask him what his business was, nor did she give him her usual snooty look down her snub nose, but opened the big double doors to Nelson's war room straight away. 'Someone very foxifluous, Generalissimo,' she announced in her fluffily-buffily voice, rapping her staff three times on the floor.

Nelson looked up from the map table where he was discussing the Queen's return to London from Scotland and her imminent visit to a dog-food factory in Wales. Horatio, who was sitting in his usual place in the armchair, telling Belle de Paw how he had once been chased by a corgi in the palace and was forced to hide in the King's sock drawer, peered over his spectacles.

Belle de Paw turned to the fox and knew instinctively that he had news about Shylo. They were all very fond of the little rabbit and were missing him dreadfully. He'd been gone for almost three days now. Belle de Paw had even sneaked into his bedroom and sat on his bed to feel close to him. However, it had only made her miss him more. Although that's a secret she would prefer you didn't tell anyone.

'I have a letter from Shylo,' ST-BT announced in his superior voice.

Nelson hobbled over, leaning on his stick. His face was very grey and his back was bent from age, but he was as sharp as he always had been. 'If Shylo has taken the trouble to get a letter to us, it must be important.'

ST-BT gave the letter to the Generalissimo then settled into the sofa opposite Horatio and crossed his long legs.

Nelson slowly lowered himself into a chair and read it. He nodded, grunted, then nodded again. He took off his spectacles.

'Shylo needs information on an American rabbit called Harlequin who has assembled hundreds of rabbits on the farm where he lives to search for the

Golden Carrot, which Harlequin believes is buried there. Apparently, he has an ancient map which tells him so. Shylo adds that this Harlequin claims to have found the map in a museum, in part of King Arthur's wall from Camelot, which was on display. He says he wouldn't have bothered us about it had it not been for that small piece of information about the wall. He says Horatio will know what it means.'

Laser went over to the telephone. 'I'll ask Rappaport to see what he can find out about this Harlequin.' She dialled the number for the rabbit whose office was at the very bottom of The Grand Burrow where he sat, staring at computer screens and surfing the internet, searching out evil plots. For the Royal Rabbits' duty was not simply to protect the Royal Family but the world too.

Horatio shook his head and steepled his paws. 'The Golden Carrot! Dark times are coming.'

'How dark, Horatio?' asked Nelson.

'I have a whole book on the Golden Carrot at home in my burrow on the farm,' said Horatio with satisfaction - he was very proud of his library. 'Rabbits have been searching for it since the time of King Arthur,' he told them. 'Legend says that it was made in the Earth's molten core by the Rabbit God, Lappin, and given to Arthur as a reward for declaring cottage pie the national dish rather than rabbit pie. Apparently, it gives the holder magical powers and eternal life.

'King Arthur was afraid that, if it got into the wrong hands, it could be used for evil. So he buried it somewhere in England, a long way from his castle, and drew a map so that he could find it again if he needed to. Shylo's information would not be of interest were it not for the mention of the castle wall. Only a handful of books claimed that Arthur hid the map there and

I have one in my burrow. Shylo has read it, which is why he recognizes its importance, and I assume that this Harlequin has read one too.

'Shylo's right. That piece of information about the map being found in a brick supposedly once part of King Arthur's castle suggests that the map is real. In which case, the chances of Harlequin finding the legendary carrot are quite high.'

'You rabbits with your legends of golden carrots,' said ST-BT with a chuckle, shaking his head in amusement.

'Does the Golden Carrot really exist?' asked Laser, turning up her nose. It all sounded like a lot of garbage to her.

'There are many who believe in it,' murred Horatio. 'Rabbits have spent their entire lives looking for it. Some will do anything for power.'

'I suppose this Harlequin wants to live forever,' said

Nelson with a sigh. 'How very unoriginal.'

'Is the carrot made of real gold?' asked Belle de Paw, who loved jewellery more than anything else (and stole the odd bauble from the Queen's dressing table when no one was looking). Her brown eyes gleamed at the thought of it.

Suddenly, Frisby opened the big doors and announced Rappaport. The scruffy, squat rabbit hopped into Nelson's war room. He dropped the piece of paper he was holding, then, when he bent down to pick it up, his spectacles fell off and landed on the floor with a clatter. When he stood up, he revealed an orange stain from breakfast on his tie and a hole in his jacket, at the elbow. He replaced his spectacles and turned the piece of paper the right way round.

'You asked about Harlequin. Well, he's wanted all over America for all sorts of things, including theft and kidnapping. He's obsessed with finding the

111

Golden Carrot . . .'

At that moment, Clooney and Zeno threw open the doors without waiting to be announced.

Frisby was furious. 'You know you can't do that! You can't just barge in. I have to announce you!' But no one was listening to her.

'Ah, Zeno, Clooney. Just in time,' said Nelson, standing up stiffly. 'You're going to Northamptonshire.'

'Are we?' asked Clooney smoothly, straightening his bow tie.

'What's in Northamptonshire?' asked Zeno.

'You're going to Shylo's farm,' he told them. 'Shylo needs our help.'

'If you're sending Zeno and Clooney to Northamptonshire, then I'm going too,' said Belle de Paw. 'If Shylo is in trouble, I should be there!'

'Ditto to that,' exclaimed Laser. 'I'm in, even though this Golden Carrot stuff sounds a little ridiculous.'

Horatio looked at her gravely. 'If the map is real and this Harlequin character finds the Golden Carrot, you won't think it ridiculous at all. That kind of power in the wrong hands is potentially catastrophic.'

Nelson nodded. 'My brother's right. We can survive here without you all for a short while, but I want you back in one piece for the King and Queen of Holland's state visit. That's just four days away. Laser and Belle de Paw can explain the situation on the way.'

Horatio stood up stiffly. 'I'm going too,' he declared.

The rabbits all turned to the old buck in bewilderment.

'I need to refer to a book in my library: *The Quest for the Golden Carrot* by Ivor Parsley. There might be something important in there that will be relevant to this case.'

'Very well,' said Nelson, shaking his head. He knew he was powerless to stop his brother once he'd got an idea in his head. 'You'd better all go right away.' He turned to ST-BT. 'Might you have time for a drink?'

The fox grinned. 'Butterscotch on the Rocks?' he asked, stroking a whisker. 'I always have time for that!'

## CHAPTER ELEVEN

A couple of days after he had ventured to the Fox & Fox, Shylo was in the field, gathering grains of wheat, and wondering yet again if Riot had managed to get his message to ST-BT. It was early afternoon and the sun was already throwing long shadows across the stubble.

Harlequin's camp now filled the forest. The news that they were hunting for the Golden Carrot had got around and new rabbits seemed to be arriving every day. Rabbits were all over the farm, digging in the fields, in the forest, on the tracks and even in Farmer Ploughman's garden. Eight had already been eaten by one of Farmer Ploughman's dogs and dozens picked off by foxes. Birds of prey circled above and Farmer Ploughman had begun to ride out on his quad bike with his gun. He was a very fine shot.

Suddenly, a fox stalked out of the hedgerow, stirring Shylo from his thoughts and sending him into a terrible panic. But then he let out a loud sigh of relief as he recognized this elegant creature in the red jacket with gold buttons.

Riot crossed the field and stopped in front of Shylo. 'Good news,' she growled softly. 'I got the message to ST-BT and he went straight to The Grand Burrow. It turns out you were right to be suspicious. Harlequin's a crook and he has to be stopped.' She swept her eyes over the holes the Magic Rabbits had dug in the field the day before. 'Looks like no one's found the

Golden Carrot yet?'

'No. I'm not sure it even exists.'

She shook her head. 'Some creatures will believe anything! But that wasn't the good news, by the way.'

'Oh? There's more?'

'Yes, your Royal Rabbit friends are coming to help you.'

Shylo's ears sprang up with excitement. 'The Hopsters? They're coming *here*?'

'They're *all* coming. You've even got the old one - what's his name? Horace? I'm going to enjoy watching the spectacle.' She grinned slyly. 'Then, when the battle's over, I think I might take Harlequin for myself. He looks like he's got a bit of fat on him.'

Shylo wondered how he would explain the appearance of the Royal Rabbits in the Warren ... Could he pretend they worked with him on the beetroot farm? After all, they had red paws as well,

'Do you know when they're arriving?' he asked.

'Apparently, they're coming down with an Amazon package guaranteed to arrive on the farm tomorrow. Really, the things they come up with in The Grand Burrow!' She grinned and her eyes gleamed. 'Personally, I'd rather ride behind ST-BT on his Harley-Davidson.'

'Thank you, Riot. I owe you,' Shylo murred.

'You owe me nothing, Shylo. I'm happy to do something for a rabbit such as you.' She put a paw on his shoulder. 'You're brave and you have a big heart. And that's what really counts, the size of your heart, not how strong you are. If you need anything else, leave me a note in the hollow tree so you don't have to come back to the Fox & Fox.'

Shylo nodded. He knew the hollow tree. He used to play in it when he was a kitten.

Riot gave him a salute and winked. 'See you, Shylo.' Then she turned and lolloped back across the field.

Shylo didn't have long to wait until the Hopsters arrived. He had to hurry and refine his plan.

It was going to be dangerous, but weren't *all* plans dangerous?

It was going to be difficult, but weren't *all* plans difficult?

There was no guarantee that it would work, but what plans *were* guaranteed to work?

When Shylo got home, he sat down at the kitchen table with a piece of paper and a pencil to work out his plan:

# SHYLO'S VERY CLEVER PLAN

## REQUIREMENTS:

5 CARROTS    1 POT OF GOLD PAINT
5 PAINTBRUSHES    A SECRET SHED TO PAINT IN

**EASY BITS:**    NONE

**HARD BITS:**    THE ONLY PLACE TO FIND CARROTS IS IN FARMER PLOUGHMANS GARDEN. REMEMBER HE HAS DOGS AND A GUN.

**HARDER BITS:**    WHERE TO FIND GOLD PAINT? TRY IN FARMER PLOUGHMANS WORKSHOP. FAILING THAT, TRY THE CHILDREN'S PLAYROOM.

**FINALE:**    REQUIRES HOPSTERS AND FOXES – MOST SPECIFICALLY, RIOT. HARLEQUIN MUST BELIEVE THAT THE PAINTED CARROT HAS REAL POWER, EVEN OVER FOXES. THEN WE HAVE TO SOMEHOW REVEAL HIM TO BE A FAKE IN FRONT OF ALL HIS MAGIC RABBITS. THIS IS GOING TO BE DIFFICULT.

**HOW CAN IT BE DONE?**    NOT SURE

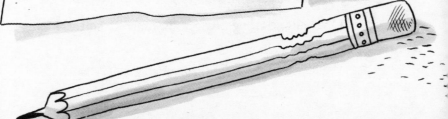

Shylo hid his plan beneath his mattress and sat on the edge of his bed. Maximilian and Elvira had totally fallen for Harlequin's fake charm and, by digging for the mysterious Golden Carrot, were putting themselves in danger. There was a strong possibility that they could be eaten by a bird of prey, a dog, or shot by Farmer Ploughman. Shylo had to convince his siblings to return to the Warren. That's where they belonged. Following Harlequin was not going to make them happy.

But Maximilian and Elvira were still not home by nightfall. They didn't return for supper, nor did they return at bedtime. They didn't come back at all.

Shylo decided to go to the mouth of the Burrow and wait for them. But instead he found his mother there, sitting beneath the stars, rubbing her paws together anxiously.

'Oh, hello, darling Shylo,' she murred softly.

'Hello, Mother,' he replied, sitting on the dewy grass beside her. 'What are you doing here?'

'Thinking,' she said and sighed as if she carried the weight of the sky with all its stars and planets on her shoulders. 'Young rabbits have always been rebellious. There's nothing new about that. And it's natural for Maximilian and Elvira to want to do things on their own. But I have an uneasy feeling in the pit of my stomach that won't go away.'

'It's called a niggle,' Shylo told her.

'A niggle?'

'It's a feeling that something's not right. I get them all the time. It can also be hunger, of course. It's hard to tell sometimes.'

'I just wish this Harlequin would move on so that our lives can go back to normal again.'

'I don't think he's going to go on his own,' said Shylo. 'But I have a plan that might work.'

'You do?' Her eyes brightened a moment before dimming again. 'You won't be in any danger, will you, Shylo?'

'You have to trust me.'

'This Golden Carrot hunt is ridiculous,' said Mrs Tawny-Tail. 'It's only a legend.'

Shylo laughed. 'I know - it seems silly. But I don't think it's really about the Golden Carrot. It's about rabbits wanting to feel special. To feel they belong.'

'But Maximilian and Elvira belong here, with us.'

'And that's what we need to tell them.'

She ran a paw down his face and gazed at him tenderly. 'When did you get so wise, little Shylo? It seems you came home just when I needed you most.'

'I hope I can help.'

'I know you can,' she said, her eyes big and trusting. 'Out of all my kittens, I believe in you the most.'

'And I believe in myself,' he replied. 'Just like you told me to.'

But Maximilian and Elvira did not come home the following morning either. They were lost - lost to Harlequin.

## CHAPTER TWELVE

Horatio's burrow was situated on the other side of the forest to the Warren - which was now not too far from where Harlequin and his growing number of followers had set up camp. Many years ago, when Horatio had escaped from the Kennel where the Queen's corgis (known as the Pack) had nearly torn him limb from limb, he'd decided to leave London and hide away in the countryside for a time.

No rabbit had ever escaped the Kennel and, even though he was a Royal Rabbit, being mauled by dogs is enough to steal any rabbit's courage, so for a long time Horatio had vanished into hiding on the farm. But, because he was an unusually large and intelligent buck, with a missing hind paw and a long, deep scar down the side of his face, the Elders of the Warren had been immediately afraid of Horatio and, without taking the trouble to get to know him, had banished him from their community and forbidden any rabbit to stray over to his side of the forest.

Horatio didn't return to The Grand Burrow for many, many years – his fear was too great and his courage was too small. Instead, he remained on the farm, alone and lonely ... until Shylo found him and became his friend, because Shylo was a curious, courageous bunkin.

And this is where Shylo waited now. Outside Horatio's burrow. The very same place he had once visited every day to listen to the old buck reading him stories from one of his books, *The Rise and Fall of the Great Rabbit Empire*, before Shylo had been sent to London by Horatio to find the Royal Rabbits.

Shylo leaned against a tree, mesmerized by the shimmering flecks of light that danced around him, and waited for the Royal Rabbits to arrive. He could hear the distant chanting, '*The time is now*,' of Harlequin's Magic Rabbits. Beside him rested a sack of food, in case his friends were hungry when they arrived, and he had his plan in his pocket.

Shylo was excited that the Hopsters would soon be here. Leaving The Grand Burrow had made him realize just how fond he was of the Royal Rabbits and he couldn't wait to see his friends. He also needed their help with his plan.

He waited and waited. The sun climbed higher in the sky. Bees buzzed and butterflies fluttered and gradually Shylo felt his eyes droop as he fell asleep...

He dreamed of a giant golden carrot rising out of the ground like a tower and Maximilian, Elvira and his other siblings dancing round it with Harlequin and his followers, all in a frenzy of devotion. It was a deeply disturbing dream and Shylo awoke with a start.

Standing in front of him, and looking down at him like five big trees blocking out the light, were Horatio, Zeno, Clooney, Laser and Belle de Paw.

Instantly forgetting his dream, Shylo jumped to his hind paws with happiness.

'You came!' he cried. 'You really came!'

He found himself enveloped in strong, affectionate arms. 'Of course we came!' murred Belle de Paw, squeezing Shylo the tightest.

'What did I teach you about trust?' said Clooney.

'You haven't forgotten you're a Royal Rabbit, have you?' boomed Zeno. 'Because you're a MONSTER!' Which was the highest compliment Zeno could give another rabbit.

'I'm glad to see my burrow's still here,' said Horatio. 'Not taken over by a squirrel or a badger, I hope?'

'It's fine,' murred Shylo. 'And I've been waiting all morning. What took you so long?'

They looked from at each other, a little embarrassed. Finally, Horatio spoke for them. 'Let's just say Royal Rabbits aren't used to the countryside. Or travelling by Guaranteed Next-day Delivery.' He chuckled. 'But we're here now. Let's go down, shall we? I need to rest my old legs.' He winked at Shylo. 'Good to be home, eh?'

'Very good,' Shylo said and they hopped down the tunnel to Horatio's burrow, deep beneath the ground.

Horatio's burrow was just as he'd left it. Simple but cosy, with shelves of beloved books, a fireplace waiting to be lit, and a big, tatty armchair where the old buck used to sit and warm his toes while Shylo sat on the stool and listened as he read to him.

'Make yourselves at home,' murred Horatio.

Shylo put his sack down on the table.

'Ah, food!' shouted Zeno, rubbing his paws together. 'Muscles don't work if you don't feed them!'

They'd told Shylo of their adventure from London to the Warren: once their package had been delivered to the farm, Belle de Paw had nearly been caught by Farmer Ploughman because she had insisted on wearing a bright pink velvet jumpsuit and Zeno had skidded on a cowpat on his way up the hill to the forest, while Laser had been stabbed by a blackberry bush as she tried to pick them.

Shylo stifled a giggle as he imagined the Hopsters he admired being so clumsy and accident-prone - they were city rabbits through and through. But they swiftly moved on to the matter at hand: Harlequin and the Golden Carrot.

Horatio took a big, dusty book from the shelf and sat down. The Hopsters pulled up chairs and gathered round him. Shylo perched on his stool just as he used to. Clooney filled Shylo in on the information Rappaport had found out about Harlequin, while Horatio scanned the big book for anything that might be helpful.

'It says that the Golden Carrot has many magical properties,' said Horatio, studying a page through his spectacles. 'But the most interesting thing about it is this: depending on the nature of the creature who has it, it can either be a force for good, or a force for evil.'

'Are you suggesting that you believe there really is a Golden Carrot buried somewhere in England?' asked Laser, still unable to believe such a silly-sounding story.

Horatio looked at her gravely. 'One must never dismiss a legend,' he growled. 'And besides it doesn't really matter whether it's real or not. It matters what rabbits *believe*. If they *believe* it will give Harlequin power, then they'll allow him to control them, and *that* is a *very* dangerous thing. You only have to look at the human world for examples of that. Throughout history, people have committed terrible crimes because of total belief in one bad person. Harlequin and his followers could set out to destroy everyone who doesn't believe in his ways. And, if the Golden Carrot *is* real, then the power it would give to Harlequin would be even more dangerous.'

Clooney looked at Shylo and grinned. 'If it was a simple dispute between your little community and another, we'd be dining on honey and gooseberry pancakes at The Grand Burrow by now, not chewing old carrots in Horatio's burrow.' He took a bite of his rather

dry carrot and chewed hard and unenthusiastically.
'But we have to assume the Golden Carrot is real. If
it falls into the wrong hands, we'll all be in danger.'

'We need a plan!' shouted Zeno, who could
never keep his voice down, even in Horatio's small
sitting room.

'Yes,' agreed Laser. 'Any ideas?'

'We have to find the Golden Carrot before
Harlequin!' Belle de Paw exclaimed. 'I do so love gold!'

'That, of course, is a genius idea!' said Clooney in
a sarcastic voice, rolling his eyes.

'Well, *you* think of a better one then!' Belle de Paw
retorted grumpily.

'We fight!' boomed Zeno, punching his paw into
his palm. 'Just give me the word and I'll call for my
Thumpers!'

'No, we need a subtler plan,' said Horatio calmly.
He took off his spectacles and looked down at Shylo,

who was sitting very quietly on the stool, staring at the piece of paper he'd pulled out of his jacket pocket. 'What have you got there?' he asked.

Shylo raised his eye a little nervously, suddenly rather unsure. 'A plan,' he murred softly.

'A plan?' the Hopsters said in unison, turning to the little rabbit.

'It requires carrots, gold paint, cunning …' Shylo paused, laying the crumpled piece of paper on the table and smoothing it out. 'And working as a team.'

'*Oh là là*,' murred Belle de Paw excitedly. 'We are always at our best when we work as a team!'

# CHAPTER THIRTEEN

Maximilian and Elvira were very pleased with themselves, for they had managed to convince two of their other siblings, Willow and Wilton, to join Harlequin's Magic Rabbits. Harlequin was delighted, and Maximilian and Elvira hoped that, as a reward, they would be invited to become Golden Rabbits. Harlequin wanted as many rabbits as possible to join him so that there would be more paws to dig for the Golden Carrot. There were now hundreds of followers, scattered all over the three thousand acres of Farmer Ploughman's land.

The four Tawny-Tail siblings hopped about the field at the edge of the wood, digging great big holes along with a dozen other followers, aware that Harlequin was watching, with Peasie the weasel, from the cool shade of an old oak. Every rabbit searching the fields hoped that they would be the one to find the Golden Carrot for Harlequin and become his favourite Magic Rabbit. There were rumours flying around the followers of what would happen once they found the Golden Carrot. Maybe Harlequin would even become as powerful as those superheroes in comic books: Super-Rabbit, Spider-Buck and Cat-Doe.

Willow heard the rumbling of a motor first. She stood on her hind legs and narrowed her eyes. She could just make out something moving along one of the farm tracks at the other end of the field, but quickly dismissed it. Tractors and other farm vehicles

were often moving round the fields and they didn't harm rabbits unless one happened to get under a wheel, which they did their very best to avoid.

The noise stopped and Willow began to dig again. All was quiet, eerily quiet. Suddenly she had a horrid thought. Could the rumble have been Farmer Ploughman's quad bike? Fearful that there was danger in the air, Willow thumped her hind paw on the ground - the warning signal that all rabbits know. When rabbits hear that sound, they don't wait around to see what it's for. THEY RUN. And that's just what most of the Magic Rabbits in the field did, as fast as they could, hopping away quickly to take cover in the nearby hedges.

Harlequin stood up and squinted into the sun. He didn't see what the fuss was about and commanded the rabbits to go back to work. They looked at him uncertainly. If Harlequin was ordering them to go back into the field, there really couldn't be any danger, could there? But still they hesitated ...

Maximilian, however, was much too focused on his digging to run; he was determined to be the rabbit to find the Golden Carrot. He also wanted Harlequin to see how fearless he was, remaining in the field when the other rabbits had fled. So, while his brother and sisters hid among the leaves, Maximilian remained, alone and quite exposed, in the middle of the field.

*BANG!*

It only took one shot. Maximilian flopped to the earth without a sound.

Willow, Wilton and Elvira stared in horror as Farmer Ploughman came into view on his quad bike. He looked around and fired his gun again. Another rabbit, also too eager to find the Golden Carrot, fell into the stubble at the other end of the field. Satisfied that he'd shot two of the annoying rabbits who had suddenly grown in number and were digging up his fields, Farmer Ploughman strode across the field to pick them up. Mrs Ploughman would be very pleased with this addition to her stockpot. They'd all enjoy a good dinner tonight.

'We can't let him take Maximilian!' cried Willow tearfully. 'We have to get him.'

'We can't!' said Elvira. 'Farmer Ploughman will shoot us as well.'

Wilton looked at Harlequin hopefully. 'Harlequin's magic!' he cried with relief, turning his gaze to the ginger rabbit, who wasn't looking at all concerned. 'He'll help us, won't you, Harlequin?'

But Harlequin had no intention of putting himself in danger. 'I reserve my magic for more important things. Leave him!' he commanded, backing away into the trees, with Peasie following hurriedly after. 'That courageous rabbit has died bravely for our cause.

He's a true Magic Rabbit. But you mustn't let anything distract you from your quest. Get back out there at once and dig, dig, dig! Be brave. Feel the magic-ragic.'

Elvira was so shocked she remained rooted to the spot. She had believed Harlequin cared for them. She'd believed he was magic.

Wilton and Willow ignored Harlequin. 'Hurry!' said Wilton. 'We only have a minute before Farmer Ploughman comes this way to pick up Maximilian.' And with surprising courage the two small rabbits scampered out, leaving Elvira trembling in the hedge. When they reached their brother, they found, to their relief, that he was still breathing.

Wilton took Maximilian's arms and Willow grabbed his legs and together they tried to drag him across the stubble to the safety of the hedgerow. But he was bigger than them and heavy too, and they simply weren't strong enough to carry him.

Elvira watched from the hedge. She had always tried to look brave because she wanted to impress Maximilian, when really she was just as scared as any other rabbit who fears being shot by a farmer. But now she was so furious with Harlequin for leaving her brother in the field that she took a deep breath and darted out.

Farmer Ploughman had picked up the other rabbit and was carrying it, by its hind paws, across the field.

Elvira knew they didn't have much time. 'Give me a leg!' she cried, seizing Maximilian's left paw. 'Now heave!'

Farmer Ploughman stopped walking and blinked. Could his eyes be deceiving him? Were three little rabbits trying to drag another one across the stubble?

He dropped the rabbit he was carrying and pulled two cartridges out of his pocket. One by one, and quickly because Farmer Ploughman was a very experienced shot, he slipped them into the slots in his gun, and shut it with a click. He took aim. He still couldn't believe what he was seeing. His finger hesitated on the trigger. Then he pulled it.

*BANG!*

But he was too late. Together, Wilton, Willow and Elvira had pulled Maximilian into the bushes and the bullet whizzed past Willow's ear, grazing off a small patch of fur as it went.

When the three rabbits stumbled into the Warren, carrying their brother, they cried for help. Rabbits popped out of the bushes and trees and up from the ground and hurried to their aid.

A couple of bucks took over and carried the wounded bunny back to the Tawny-Tail Burrow.

Mrs Tawny-Tail was preparing tea when they

staggered down the tunnel. As she took in the bucks'
serious faces and saw what they were carrying, her
blood turned cold. Her husband had been shot by
Farmer Ploughman when her kittens were small.

They laid Maximilian on his bed. Mrs Tawny-Tail
hurried to fetch water and towels and set about
tending to the wound in his side. Maximilian lay with
his eyes closed.

'Please don't let him die!' she sobbed to the Great
Rabbit in the sky. 'Please don't take him from me as
you took his father.'

When Shylo returned to the Burrow that evening, he
found the atmosphere tense and sombre.

His family were gathered round Maximilian's bed
and his brother lay in bandages.

'What happened?' Shylo asked, hopping into the

room in alarm.

'We were digging for the Golden Carrot,' said Willow with a sniff. 'Farmer Ploughman shot him.'

Immediately, Shylo knew what to do. 'I know just the rabbit who can help,' he declared and hurried out of the Burrow without a backward glance.

When he returned a short while later, he was accompanied by the biggest rabbit any of the others had ever seen.

'Don't be afraid,' Zeno said to the alarmed Tawny-Tail family, in an unusually soft voice for him. He glanced at Shylo. 'I work with Shylo on the beetroot farm and we get the occasional gunshot wound there. Let me take a look and see if we can get this young bunkin on his feet again.'

The rabbits stood aside to let him pass. They couldn't take their eyes off him. Wilton stared at the enormous buck's arms and wondered how *he* could get muscles like that. Willow saw the red stain on his paw, like Shylo's, and wondered why beetroots only dyed one paw and not two.

Zeno unwrapped the bandages. He nodded at Shylo and Shylo smiled encouragingly at his mother. He was right. Zeno knew exactly what to do.

## CHAPTER FOURTEEN

The following morning, Maximilian opened his foggy eyes and blinked at the anxious faces of his family, who were standing round his bed. 'What happened?' he murred.

'You were shot,' said Wilton.

'By Farmer Ploughman!' exclaimed Willow.

'We thought you were dead,' murred Elvira in a quiet voice. 'Harlequin watched you fall and did nothing to help you. He's not the Magic Rabbit we thought he was, Maximilian. He's a liar.'

There was a long pause as the memories of the day before slowly returned to Maximilian.

'Your brother and sisters were very brave,' his mother told him, running a gentle paw over his forehead. 'They carried you all the way home.'

'Farmer Ploughman wanted you for the pot!' Wilton informed him.

'He was going to make you into a stew,' said Willow.

'But we weren't going to let that happen,' added Elvira fiercely.

'Shylo brought a friend who treated your wound. It's thanks to him that you're alive. We nearly lost you,' said his mother.

Wilton grinned broadly. 'His friend is *really* big and *really* muscly and I'm going to be as big and muscly as him one day.'

'He has a red paw just like Shylo,' Lewie added. 'Because he works on the beetroot farm.'

Maximilian looked at each face in turn. Wilton, Willow, Elvira, Erica, Lewie and his mother. 'Where's Shylo?' he asked.

'He left at the crack of dawn,' said Mrs Tawny-Tail.

Maximilian closed his eyes and drifted off to sleep. He dreamed of a big golden carrot. It shone brightly, promising him a place in Harlequin's Golden Circle. Suddenly, the head of a little worm appeared, burrowing out of the carrot. Then another, and another, until finally hundreds of little worms were wiggling out of the gold, filling it with holes, until there was nothing left.

The Hopster rabbits wasted no time in getting to work on Shylo's plan. First they needed to steal some gold paint from Farmer Ploughman's workshop. This was not easy because not only did Farmer Ploughman have vicious dogs but there were cats on the farm, to eat the mice and rats, and they loved eating rabbits, if they were quick enough to catch one.

Second they needed to steal some big carrots from Farmer Ploughman's vegetable garden. This wasn't going to be easy either because Farmer Ploughman's wife had put up wire netting all round the vegetable garden to keep the rabbits out. And, now that there were suddenly so many rabbits on the farm, she had also taken to guarding her precious vegetable garden with a shotgun of her own (and she was a better shot than her husband).

Third they needed a secret place to paint, for Horatio's burrow was not big enough and he certainly didn't want gold paint splattered all over his walls! Horatio remembered once coming across the gamekeeper's old shed, which hadn't been used in a very long time, and he set off with Laser to find it again so they could make sure it didn't have any unwelcome residents who might get in the way of their preparations.

Shylo led Belle de Paw, Zeno and Clooney to the post and rail fence that separated the fields of the farm from the main farmhouse and buildings. It was easy to hop through.

'Clooney and I will look for paint in the workshop,' boomed Zeno, who didn't like to take orders from anyone but the Generalissimo and certainly not from a little bunny from the countryside (even if he had come up with the plan). 'You and Belle de Paw dig up the carrots,' he added. 'It'll take a small rabbit to sneak through a hole in the wire netting around the vegetable patch.'

'My teeth are sharp enough to gnaw through that,' murred Belle de Paw, grinning at Shylo. 'Then I will wait for you to bring me the carrots.'

Shylo thought of Mrs Ploughman and her shotgun and he felt so frightened he had to concentrate very hard on keeping his ears erect. One was very close to drooping over his eyepatch and exposing his lack of courage. Then he thought of Maximilian lying wounded in bed, and of all the other rabbits who were being drawn under Harlequin's spell, and knew that he *could* be brave ... that he *must* be brave.

'Good luck! We'll meet you back at Horatio's burrow as soon as we can!' Clooney said, and, before Shylo could even reply, Zeno and he had jumped through the rails in the fence and were scampering across the open ground to hide in the bushes growing to the side of one of the barns.

'Come on, Shylo,' encouraged Belle de Paw, perhaps noticing that he looked a little queasy. 'We're a team and we will work together. The farmer's wife is no match for us!'

Shylo felt a bit better. He *was* a Royal Rabbit and he could do this. He hopped under the railing while Belle de Paw launched herself through the gap above.

With his eyes darting from left to right (wary of cats and dogs) and stopping occasionally to take cover, he led Belle de Paw round the side of the farmhouse and up the garden until they reached the greenhouse next to a large vegetable patch bursting with autumn delights.

But, to his dismay, Mrs Ploughman was on her hands and knees on the other side of the wire netting, pulling up potatoes and tossing them into a basket. Her wicker chair was placed in the corner, beside a raspberry bush, and her shotgun was leaning up against it. One of her dogs was lying on the lawn with its eyes shut.

'The dog is asleep,' whispered Belle de Paw. 'We mustn't wake him.'

'And we mustn't disturb Mrs Ploughman either.'

'I will gnaw a small hole in the wire netting for you to squeeze through. You dig up the carrots as fast as you can and pass them to me through the hole. Understand?'

'By will or by luck,' murred Shylo with a small smile. He knew there was a good chance he would not make it out alive.

'With a moist carrot and a wet nose,' added Belle de Paw. 'Let's go.'

Meanwhile, Clooney and Zeno had made it into the workshop. There were so many pieces of machinery, cupboards full of dusty bottles and jars of liquids, that the two Hopsters didn't know where to look first. They decided to start at opposite ends of the room.

They needed paint and brushes and they needed them fast. It was only a matter of time before a farm cat picked up their scent and came along to see what was going on.

The two rabbits worked swiftly and efficiently, as one would expect Royal Rabbits to do. They might not have been used to the countryside, but they were sharp-witted, intelligent rabbits who learned fast. It didn't take them long to find some brushes. Zeno, who was balancing on a narrow shelf, lifted up a whole jar, which contained five big brushes, recently cleaned. He turned to Clooney who was standing on a table, gazing at himself in the reflection of a silver pot of paint.

'You going to admire yourself all morning or are you going to look for the paint?' boomed Zeno crossly.

Clooney didn't react. He remained very still, staring into the silver. 'Don't move a muscle,' he said in a calm, steady voice.

Zeno understood at once. Clooney had seen something else besides his reflection in the silver. Zeno turned his eyes to the floor where a sleek black cat was sitting, watching them with large green eyes.

'Have you found the paint?' Zeno said to Clooney while remaining as still as a statue.

'I've found paint, not *the* paint,' Clooney replied, running his eyes over the labels on the pots lined up against the wall. There was red and blue and yellow, but no gold.

Carefully, Zeno put down the jar of brushes. 'It's about time I used these muscles,' he said. 'I'm not the Marshal of the Thumpers because I hide from cats! Hurry up and find the paint. I'm going to play.'

And with that he jumped to the ground.

The cat got to her feet, tail in the air, as stiff as a pole.

Zeno grinned. 'My lady, may I have the next dance?'

The cat sprang.

# CHAPTER FIFTEEN

All the while Belle de Paw gnawed at the wire, Shylo stared at the dog. Its belly went gently up and down as it breathed and occasionally it paddled its feet in a dream, but it didn't wake up. It had no reason to. All was quiet. The sun was shining and the dog slumbered contentedly in the warmth of the early autumn rays.

At last, the hole was big enough for Shylo to squeeze through. Belly to the ground and making sure he was hidden behind a row of orange pumpkins, he made his way to the line of carrots.

He was just about to dig up his first one when he sensed movement behind him. The fur on his neck bristled. His heart stopped. But, when nothing bad happened, he turned round slowly. There, to his surprise, was a mole.

Shylo breathed out with relief.

'I think I must have made a wrong turning,' said the mole, peering at Shylo through her thick spectacles. (Moles, as I'm sure you know, are nearly blind, but those lucky enough to have glasses can see a little.)

'Where were you hoping to be?' Shylo asked. Just because he was in a great hurry didn't mean he should forget his manners.

'I was aiming for the compost heap at the other end of the garden,' said the mole, licking her lips with a pointy pink tongue. 'There are lots of worms and woodlice there.'

'This is the vegetable patch,' Shylo informed her politely.

'Ah, then I *have* taken a wrong turning. Thanks for your help!' With that, the mole disappeared down her hole, leaving Shylo alone once more to get on with his task.

He dug rapidly and energetically. When he had pulled up his first carrot, he hurried back to the hole in the wire netting and handed it to Belle de Paw.

'*Magnifique!* Belle de Paw exclaimed, beaming. 'But we need HUGE ones! The biggest you can find!'

Encouraged by her praise, Shylo went to dig up more. He figured he needed four or five, just in case they made mistakes. In order for the carrot to be passed off as the *real* Golden Carrot, it had to be perfect and very large.

A moment later, Shylo passed the second carrot to Belle de Paw. Then the third, then the fourth. Really, this was much easier than he'd anticipated. He was in the middle of digging up the fifth when he heard a high-pitched squeal erupt from the lawn.

He stood on his hind legs to see what was going on.

The Ploughmans' youngest daughter was standing on the grass, pointing at a mound of earth. The mole, who had only a moment ago been in the vegetable garden, now poked out her head and looked around hopefully.

'Oh no!' she groaned in disappointment. 'Wrong again!' And she proceeded to disappear back into the mound of earth and head for the other end of the garden before the girl had time to grab her.

To Shylo's dismay, the commotion had awoken the dog. It trotted to the mound of earth and sniffed it excitedly, wagging its tail. The girl patted it.

'If you hadn't been asleep, you might have caught the mole,' she said. 'Useless dog!' Then she turned to her mother, who was now on her feet. 'We need to set a mole trap, Mum.'

With the mole now vanished into the ground, the dog grew bored of the mound of earth and looked around to see what else might be on offer in the garden. Instantly, it spotted Belle de Paw by the fence. It pricked its ears, narrowed its eyes and immediately gave chase.

Belle de Paw scampered as quickly as she could towards the hedge, desperately trying not to drop the carrots Shylo had collected. But the dog was fast and Belle de Paw was slowed down by her load. She could almost smell its breath (dog food, yuck!) as it was now only a whisker away . . .

Then something extraordinary happened.

Rabbits appeared everywhere, swarming in great numbers into Mr and Mrs Ploughman's garden!

As Belle de Paw dived into the hedge, the dog,

distracted by the sight of so many paws and so many white, fluffy tails and so many pairs of ears, skidded to a stop on the grass, allowing the Hopster time to make her escape without dropping a single carrot.

The rabbits in the garden began digging frantically.

The dog blinked. Was this a dream? If it was, it was quite possibly the most delightful dream ever! It jumped up and down with excitement.

*BANG!*

The farmer's wife fired her gun in an attempt to deter the digging bunnies.

Shylo, still in the middle of the vegetable garden, could only watch in horror as Mrs Ploughman fired her shotgun randomly at the magic-crazed rabbits. He grabbed the final carrot and, deciding not to risk running across the lawn, he dived into the hole the mole had made and scampered through the darkness, hoping that the mole had burrowed successfully to the compost heap, after all.

He hadn't seen Belle de Paw make it to the safety of the hedge and, as he scrabbled through the dark, he prayed that she was OK. It sickened him to think of her in the middle of all that pandemonium with Mrs Ploughman's bullets whizzing through the air and the dog in determined pursuit. But he had to trust that Belle would know what to do. She was, after all, a Royal Rabbit.

At last, when he came out into the light, he saw, to his relief, the compost heap, and the mole dining happily on juicy worms and crispy woodlice. Shylo hurried away from the garden and towards the field, carrying his carrot and trying not to listen to the sound of Mrs Ploughman's shotgun ringing through the air.

Zeno wrestled with the cat. This might sound odd to a

reader unfamiliar with these extra-large, super-intelligent, highly trained Hopster rabbits, but, to those of you in the know, you will appreciate that for Zeno a cat was not the most fearsome opponent. Ratzis, being giant super-rats, were worse, *far* worse, minks were pretty dreadful but cats, vicious and cunning as they were, did not necessarily mean curtains for a Royal Rabbit Hopster.

As Zeno and the cat tumbled and rolled, dived and ducked on the floor, Clooney swiftly read the labels on all the pots of paint lined up in a row on the wall at the back of the workshop. At last, he found the word GOLD written in large black letters on a big white label. He didn't know that not so very long ago Farmer Ploughman's son had gone to school in fancy dress - as a goldfish.

Clooney grabbed the pot and jumped to the ground. Now to put an end to the fight so that he and Zeno could escape.

Sweeping his gaze round the workshop, Clooney spotted a large basket, in the shape of a dome, lying in the corner beneath a blanket of dust. He placed the paint pot on the floor and hurried over to get it. Then, when he saw an opportune moment, he placed the basket over the cat, capturing it inside like a spider in a cup.

Zeno was very surprised to see that the cat had been trapped, and a little disappointed, for he felt he very much had the situation under control. But, without waiting for an explanation, or indeed any sort of conversation, he retrieved the brushes and together the two Royal Rabbits scampered out of the workshop before the cat had worked out how to free herself (which she did, pretty swiftly, for cats are almost as clever as Hopster rabbits).

By early afternoon, all of the Hopster rabbits had gathered once more at Horatio's burrow. Shylo was first to arrive and was relieved to see Belle de Paw a few moments later. When Zeno and Clooney appeared with the paint and brushes, the rabbits didn't congratulate each other, or celebrate their triumphs, for this was only the beginning of the plan and there was a long way to go before they could revel in their success. The group of four simply nodded in the way Royal Rabbits do when part of a plan has been completed, and set off for the gamekeeper's shed in search of Horatio and Laser.

# CHAPTER SIXTEEN

I n the quiet of the gamekeeper's shed the six Royal Rabbits set to work. Horatio and Laser washed the carrots so their skin was clean and smooth. Zeno gave them each a brush and Clooney opened the pot of gold paint. It looked delicious enough to eat, like golden syrup!

Zeno's strokes were brisk and long and paint splattered everywhere as he ran his brush up and down the carrot in a very slapdash manner.

'Hey, Zeno, easy with the paint!' snapped Laser

crossly. 'You want me covered in gold?'

Belle de Paw, who was painting with great care, smiled to herself. 'I wouldn't mind being covered in gold if it was *real* gold,' she murred.

'If you get any paint on my tuxedo, Zeno, I'll paint stripes on you so you're mistaken for a bee!' said Clooney, standing back to admire his work. It was, it must be said, very impressive.

'You'd make a very scary bee, Zeno,' said Shylo, who was really enjoying painting his carrot. 'The biggest, scariest bee in the world!'

Once they'd finished, they hung their carrots from a line of baler twine, which they'd found in the shed, like clothes on a washing line.

Horatio hobbled from one to the other, leaning on his walking stick. He observed them through his spectacles and *ummed* and *aahed* and scratched his chin. Finally, he nodded. 'Pretty good effort,' he said

174

in his deep, gravelly voice. 'Let's allow them to dry overnight and review them in the morning. But I'd say we have five very fine golden carrots to choose from. Once we've picked the most perfect golden carrot, Shylo needs to convince Harlequin that it's been found.'

He patted Shylo's head fondly. 'I don't like to think what he'll do to you if he realizes it's a fake.'

As Shylo hopped home that evening, he considered his plan. So far it had gone very well. But now he had to persuade Elvira or Maximilian to help him because he needed to know how to get Harlequin on his own. Then he had to get a message to Riot. The whole plot depended on *her*. He knew it was a brilliant idea. Probably the best idea he'd ever had. But timing was everything, and being a rather anxious bunkin meant that he feared the worst: Riot wouldn't get his message, his siblings wouldn't want to help him and, his worst fear of all, Harlequin would realize immediately that the Golden Carrot they presented to him was a fake. Oh, it could all go horribly wrong!

When he arrived home, his mother was making parsnip and carrot pie for supper. Shylo's stomach gave a groan of hunger. They'd been so busy with the plan today that he'd not eaten since his early breakfast.

'Shylo, Maximilian wants to see you,' his mother murred softly, brushing the pastry with butter.

Shylo's ear flopped over his eyepatch. He did not want to go and see Maximilian. 'I'll go after supper,' he said.

'No, my dear. He wants to see you now,' she said. 'He's been asking for you all day.'

Shylo's paws dragged across the floor as he made

his way to his brother's bedroom. He hesitated a moment at the door and reminded himself that his brother was wounded so he wouldn't be able hurt him. Then he went in.

Maximilian, who had been sleeping, opened his eyes. They brightened when he saw Shylo.

Shylo approached the bed and looked down at his brother. He looked so small and fragile beneath the quilt. 'How are you feeling?' he asked.

'Like I've been shot,' said Maximilian.

Shylo was used to his brother's sarcasm and he gave a sigh, but his brother grinned weakly. 'I want to thank you,' he said.

Shylo was surprised. Maximilian had never thanked him for anything, ever.

'Mother told me that your friend saved me. If it hadn't been for him - and you - I'd be dead.'

Shylo didn't know what to say - he wasn't used to

this new, softer tone of voice. Nor was he used to the kinder look on his brother's face.

'I want to say sorry too,' Maximilian continued. 'You were right and I was wrong. Harlequin and the Magic Rabbits aren't family, *we* are. I'm only sorry I had to be shot to realize it. Elvira, Willow and Wilton risked their lives to drag me off the field. They could have all been killed.'

He gazed at Shylo with large, shiny eyes welling with tears. 'Harlequin is a bad rabbit and I'm an idiot to have believed in him. He left me to die in the field, but you, you ...' He sniffed as a large tear trickled down his fur. 'You cared for me even though I was horrid to you.'

Shylo felt his heart expand, like it contained a bright golden light that was now radiating out to Maximilian and enveloping him. 'You're my brother,' he said shyly.

'And you're mine,' said Maximilian, looking a little

surprised himself because being nice makes you feel so much better than being mean.

Maximilian's paw appeared from beneath the quilt. He held it out to Shylo and Shylo took it.

'Once he finds the Golden Carrot, Harlequin wants to take over the Warren, the country and then the world. You have to stop him, Shylo,' Maximilian told his brother. 'And I want to help you. What can I do?'

Shylo smiled. 'You can give me some information.'

Maximilian frowned. 'You're not going to do this on your own, are you?'

Shylo grinned. 'I have some big friends from the beetroot farm who'll help me.'

'Ah, the beetroot farm. Your red paw.' Maximilian narrowed his eyes. 'Funny that the beetroots only dye one paw, and that the red doesn't come off when you wash.'

Shylo looked down at the special mark of the Royal

Rabbits, and a small smile crept across his face. 'It's a long story,' he said.

'OK, another time then,' said Maximilian. 'So tell me, what do you need to know?'

That evening, after supper, Shylo hopped over to the hollow tree to leave a message for Riot. To his surprise, the vixen was already there, leaning against the trunk and filing her claws with a broken piece of tile. 'Well, well, well, if it isn't Shylo, come to leave me a message.'

'How did you know I was coming?' Shylo asked, putting the note back in his jacket pocket.

'I didn't. The truth is I need to see *you*.'

'You do?'

'Yes.' She tossed away the tile. 'It's like this. There are now so many Magic Rabbits everywhere that it's making the foxes nervous. *I'm* not nervous. I don't *do* nervous. But the others are getting a bit twitchy. Sounds silly – I mean, rabbits are food so why complain, eh? But too many rabbits ...' She sighed and shook her head. 'Too many and we're seriously outnumbered. The other foxes have decided they want to bring down the numbers. They're planning an attack and then a big, big feast. So I wanted to warn you because I know you have family and, well, we're friends, right?'

Shylo nodded. 'I have a plan to stop Harlequin which will mean all his followers will leave, then there'll be no need for the other foxes to attack. But it involves the two of us working together,' he said.

Riot was surprised. 'Really? How?'

As Shylo told Riot his idea, a wide grin spread over her face. When he'd finished, she held up her paw.

'Happy to help,' she said, giving Shylo a high five. 'And, by the way, that's the bravest plan I ever heard!'

# CHAPTER SEVENTEEN

The following morning, Shylo left the Warren early and headed to the gamekeeper's shed to meet the Hopsters. It was an overcast day. Heavy grey-bellied clouds hung low in the sky and it looked like it would rain. Shylo was nervous. His stomach rumbled, not with hunger - he'd been careful to have a large breakfast in anticipation of the big day ahead - but with anxiety. Today was the day. Everything was in place. Now all he needed was the Golden Carrot.

He pushed open the door to the shed and saw at

once that something was wrong.

The five other Royal Rabbits were standing in front of the line of hanging carrots, looking puzzled. Shylo's heart plummeted to his feet and his mouth went dry.

The Hopster rabbits stood aside as Shylo hopped forward. Then he saw what had happened. Bugs had crawled along the baler twine in the night and climbed all over the carrots, getting stuck in the paint as it dried. They looked like ancient amber fossils of prehistoric insects. Shylo felt sick.

'What are we gonna do?' Laser demanded. 'Without our golden carrot, the plan won't work!'

'We have more paint, we just need more carrots,' suggested Clooney. 'Seeing as you were so good at getting them last time, Shylo, perhaps you'd like to dig up a few more?'

Horatio scratched his chin. 'There's no time for that. Everything is set for this afternoon. We have to return to The Grand Burrow tonight and prepare for the Dutch state visit. There must be something we can do to salvage the plan.'

He turned. 'Is there something you'd like to share with us?'

All eyes shifted to Belle de Paw. She sighed and clicked her tongue. A shadow of irritation swept across her face. Then she looked down at Shylo and the irritation passed, and in its place came compassion.

'How did you know?' she asked Horatio.

'I'm an old and wise Royal Rabbit. I make it my business to know.'

'All right,' she said, folding her arms. 'I have another golden carrot.'

They all looked at her in astonishment.

'I just wanted one to keep. They are so *pretty*, so I snuck back into the vegetable garden last night, dug up a carrot and painted it for myself.' She sighed again and turned to Horatio. 'I'll just hop back to your burrow and get it. I dried it in Horatio's airing cupboard. Needless to say, it is perfect.'

She disappeared, only to return a few minutes later with the carrot. It was, indeed, perfect and *very* golden.

Maximilian had told Shylo that at nine o'clock every morning Harlequin sent his Magic Rabbits off to dig for the Golden Carrot so that he could have some alone time to work. What work he did exactly no one knew, but they assumed he was doing something very magical and did not want to be disturbed. So, at ten past nine, Shylo and the Hopster rabbits made their way to Harlequin's camp, careful not to be seen. Horatio, who was too old and lame for this kind of action, stayed behind in his burrow, waiting for news. As the rabbits neared the camp, they took cover beneath a laurel bush to finalize the last details of the plan.

As he was used to doing before any battle, Zeno took charge, instructing the others where to position themselves. Then Shylo slipped off his jacket and wrapped it round Belle de Paw's beautifully painted golden carrot. He stood up straight and made sure his ears stood up too because he didn't want the others to see how nervous he was. But Belle de Paw touched his cheek and he knew from the tender look on her face that she sensed how very scared he was.

'With a wet nose,' murred Clooney.

'A moist carrot . . .' Laser added.

'Actually, it's gold,' Clooney whispered with a grin.

'Shhhh!' Laser snapped. 'You're ruining the moment!'

'And a slice of mad courage!' Zeno exclaimed, trying unsuccessfully to lower his voice. Then the four big Hopster rabbits put their red paws on top of each other to make a tower, to which Shylo added his own.

'Be brave, little Shylo,' Belle de Paw said. 'We have your back.'

And Shylo set off, a little hesitantly, into the empty camp.

For a bunkin with a very sensitive nose like Shylo's, Harlequin's camp was almost unbearable. It looked as if a terrible storm had passed through, but the storm was the Magic Rabbits themselves, who seemed to have lost all sense of who they really were and had clearly forgotten how to look after themselves.

Shylo picked his way past the rubbish until he got to the only tent that wasn't made of rags. This one was made of a patchwork quilt and covered a large area of ground. *It must be big enough for the Golden Rabbits to all fit in together,* Shylo mused, thinking of Maximilian and how he'd longed to be chosen. He wondered what the Golden Rabbits did in there.

Shylo pulled back the quilt and peered inside. He expected to find Harlequin busy at work, but instead he was *sleeping*!

The ginger buck was lying in a hammock, snoring loudly. Asleep, he looked fat and bloated, as if someone had filled him with water.

Shylo looked around. His eyes settled on piles of what were clearly stolen goods: small items from the farm, silver and brass household things, purses and wallets and handbags, even clothes. Shylo felt a little dizzy at the sight of such obvious evidence of thievery. Was it possible that Harlequin was using the Golden Rabbits to steal for him?

Shylo coughed. Harlequin didn't stir. Shylo coughed again.

Harlequin opened his eyes and blinked for a

moment as if slowly remembering where he was. Then he focused and saw Shylo standing nervously in the entrance of the tent, clutching something to his chest.

The ginger rabbit sat up with a start, furious to have been discovered sleeping, and worried that Shylo might have spotted all the valuable things he had made his Golden Rabbits steal for him.

'Shylo! What are you doing back here, little bro? You've interrupted my magic sleep! Recharging my magic-ragic powers,' Harlequin grumbled and suddenly Shylo saw the *real* Harlequin behind the mask. He was bad-tempered and impatient and, without his smile, he lost all of his charm.

'Forgive me for disturbing you,' Shylo murred. He walked towards the hammock and kneeled, pretending to worship Harlequin as the Magic Rabbits did. 'I believe in the magic-ragic. I believe in *you.*'

Harlequin smiled and put out his paw. Shylo

supposed he was meant to kiss it. He hesitated. The paw remained. Shylo realized he had no choice and hopped gingerly over to give it a nudge with his muzzle. It was enough.

'So you wanna be a Magic Rabbit?' said Harlequin with a grin.

'I want to be a *Golden* Rabbit,' murred Shylo. 'I've found the Golden Carrot.'

At that, Harlequin leaped out of the hammock. 'Where? Where is it? Give it to me!' His amber eyes blazed with greed.

Shylo began to unfold the jacket with great care. He moved so slowly that Harlequin grabbed it impatiently and hastily unfolded it himself. When he saw the gold, his jaw opened and he gasped, a deep, low gasp that came right from the bottom of his chest. He put his paws round the carrot and lifted it up.

'The Golden Carrot!' he gushed. Then he hopped

outside to see it in the light. Shylo followed after him, hoping that he wouldn't notice any flaws.

Harlequin, so greedy for power, was easily taken in, turning the carrot over and over, sighing and groaning with joy and triumph.

Then Shylo smelled fox. It came in an unmistakable whiff, thick and sharp and overpowering.

Harlequin was too absorbed in the Golden Carrot to notice, and, when Riot stepped into the clearing, he was so taken by surprise that he almost dropped his prize.

Riot prowled over to Harlequin and put her nose right up to his. Harlequin froze in terror, eyes bulging.

'Show her the carrot!' Shylo cried, pretending to be afraid of the fox.

Harlequin pushed the carrot out in front of him and took a deep breath.

Riot looked at it and frowned. Then she narrowed

her eyes and, all of a sudden, rolled on to her back with her legs in the air and began to meow like a kitten.

*OK, don't overdo it,* Shylo thought as Riot waved her paws, wagged her bushy tail and made strange noises, clearly enjoying the game.

'IT WORKS!' Harlequin cried.

Riot rolled on to her paws and pretended to bow down in front of the ginger rabbit. Shylo pulled a face, silently trying to tell her to back off - she could blow the whole plan ...

But he needn't have worried. Harlequin was triumphant. He had subdued a fox!

'I AM THE MOST POWERFUL CREATURE IN THE WORLD!' he yelled in triumph. The ginger rabbit pointed to the trees. 'Go, fox, and tell all your friends who's King of the Forest now!' Then he smiled at Shylo, a sly and evil smile. 'I know who you are, little rabbit. I know what that red paw of yours means. Now we've taken over the farm, we'll take over Buckingham Palace. I'm the King now! Get Peasie. Call a meeting of all the Magic Rabbits. I will rule the world! The time is NOW!'

## CHAPTER EIGHTEEN

Shylo hit the gong. Peasie clashed the cymbals. The Magic Rabbits gathered, singing and dancing and chanting, 'Follow the magic-ragic! Praise Harlequin! The time is NOW!' Harlequin appeared in front of the crowd in a gold robe that reached the ground. From a distance, it shone with glamour, but up close it was grubby and a little torn.

'My precious Magic Rabbits!' he shouted, arms outstretched in a wide embrace. He was so excited he was twitchy and jittery.

Rabbits were crammed into the clearing, stiffening their ears to hear what their leader had to say. Shylo was in the front row because Harlequin had promised him a reward for finding the Golden Carrot. He hoped Zeno, Belle de Paw, Laser and Clooney were in the trees, and - if all was going to plan - they wouldn't be alone. He tried to make them out, but saw nothing but brown trunks and red and yellow leaves.

'Today is a very special day,' shouted Harlequin in a surprisingly loud voice. '*I* have found the Golden Carrot!'

Loud applause erupted as rabbits thumped their hind paws on the ground. It was so loud the leaves on the trees began to tremble and fall.

Harlequin very slowly lifted the carrot above his head for everyone to see. The thumping stopped and the rabbits stared at it in silence and awe.

'I am now the most powerful rabbit in the world.

Nothing can stop me. Together we'll take over this farm, then this country and finally *I* will rule the world!'

The Magic Rabbits began to chant: 'Farm! Country! World!'

Harlequin held up a paw to silence them. 'The Warren is ours now, my precious Magic Rabbits. I give you its warm homes to keep you cosy this winter. Take what you want and enjoy it, and tell anyone who dares challenge you that Harlequin has given you the Warren because Harlequin is generous and good and powerful enough to provide everything you need.'

Suddenly, there came the overpowering scent of fox. It filled the clearing like smoke. The rabbits sat up in alarm and looked around in panic. Then they saw, to their horror and disbelief, foxes loping slowly out of the trees, encircling them.

But Harlequin wasn't at all concerned. He held up the Golden Carrot.

'Do not be afraid, my Magic Rabbits! See how powerful I am!' he crowed. 'See how pathetic the foxes are in the light of this mighty carrot.'

The foxes began to snarl. Their turned-up snouts creased, their eyes narrowed, the fur on the back of their necks stood up.

Then Riot strode up to Harlequin and opened her jaw wide and let out a howl, like a wolf. Harlequin's fur rippled in the force of her breath.

He stared at the carrot and frowned. Then he shook it, as if wondering why it was suddenly not working.

Shylo seized his moment. With his heart racing he hopped on to his hind paws, snatched the carrot out of Harlequin's clutches and took a bite.

The rabbits gasped.

Harlequin squealed.

Shylo took another bite. Then he spoke to the crowd. 'Harlequin is a liar!' he shouted. 'This carrot has no magical powers - it doesn't even taste that good - and it isn't real gold either!'

Harlequin stared at him in astonishment and bitter disappointment as his dream was broken between Shylo's teeth.

Out of the wood strode the four Hopster rabbits. They were so large and so fearsome that panic swept through the throng of rabbits. Laser put a paw on the whip that hung at her hip. 'Harlequin is a criminal who is wanted all over America,' she cried. 'And we're here to take him in.'

At the sound of Laser's American accent, Harlequin began to tremble. He dropped to his knees. 'I was gonna do good. I promise you, I was gonna make the world a better place. I believed in the Golden Carrot.' He pointed at Peasie. 'It was him. *He* wanted to trick everyone. You can never trust a weasel!'

The weasel jumped up and down in fury, baring his

teeth. 'Wait till I get my paws on you, you lying–!'

The foxes snarled and licked their chops.

The rabbits in the clearing began to run away, crying, 'There is no Golden Carrot! Harlequin has no power! He has no magic! He's a liar!' They darted into bushes, trees and undergrowth, anywhere they could to escape the foxes and the horror of realizing suddenly that they had put their trust in a cheat. That Harlequin had never loved *them* - he had only loved power.

Harlequin tried to flee. He pushed past the rabbits who had been so devoted to him, shoving them towards the foxes, and shouting, 'Eat *them*, not me! I'm really just a scrawny old rabbit.'

The foxes gave chase, but they had been told not to kill - and, although you may imagine foxes not to be especially loyal creatures, they're surprisingly agreeable when asked very politely, as Shylo had done.

Only *one* rabbit had been excluded from the agreement, but as Riot watched Harlequin hopping about in panic, trying to save himself, she decided that he really wasn't worth the effort. The best punishment would be to leave him to live with his failure, friendless and alone. She reckoned he wouldn't be any trouble to anyone else in the future after this. Let the Royal Rabbits capture him and send him back to America for a life in prison.

Besides, he didn't look very tasty.

Soon the clearing was empty. The Magic Rabbits had gone as quickly as they'd arrived on the farm. They hadn't bothered to take their things with them; they'd simply disappeared.

Shylo looked around at the terrible mess. The four Hopsters made their way towards him. 'We'll help tidy this up before we head back to the, er, beetroot farm,' said Laser, with a grin.

'*Oh là là*, what a job!' Belle de Paw did *not* enjoy cleaning up and would do her best to get out of it.

'You did well, Shylo,' boomed Zeno. 'You're a MONSTER!' He ruffled Shylo's fur. Shylo smiled up at him proudly.

'Yes, Shylo, you've saved your Warren,' added Clooney. 'And perhaps the world if the Golden Carrot really is buried here somewhere . . .'

Riot strode up to the rabbits. 'Shylo, could I have a moment alone?' she asked.

'Sure,' he replied.

The Hopsters left Shylo and Riot to talk and began to clear up.

Riot looked a little embarrassed. 'Hey, Shylo, I wondered if you'd put a good word in for me with ST-BT, so he'll let me ride his bike . . . will you say some nice things about me? I mean, I was pretty good today, wasn't I?'

'You really were,' said Shylo truthfully.

'I didn't overdo it?'

'You *nearly* overdid it,' he said with a smile.

'Well, you know, I'm a bit of an actress. So tell ST-BT, won't you?'

'I will,' he said.

'It was nice working with you. We should

do it again some time.'

Shylo hoped he wouldn't need to.

When Shylo returned home, it was late. The whole
Warren was celebrating. Fairy lights twinkled in the
trees like stars, and rabbits danced and sang merrily.
Though it must be said that some of the very foolish
rabbits who had chosen to follow Harlequin remained
in their burrows, feeling rather ashamed of themselves!

Shylo was about to look for his family when, to his
surprise and pleasure, *they* found *him*. His mother's
eyes filled with tears and she embraced him fiercely.
'I'm so proud of you, Shylo,' she murred.

His siblings were by her side. Maximilian, his body
wrapped in bandages, was leaning on Willow and
Erica, looking very serious. Beside him stood Wilton,
Lewie and Elvira. Facing them like this reminded Shylo

of when they used to tease him, and for a moment his heart sank. What if they were unkind to him again?

Maximilian put out his paw and Shylo caught his breath because it was coming straight for his eyepatch. But then his brother's face softened and he placed his paw very gently over Shylo's eye.

'What are you doing?' asked Shylo in a small voice.

'Making it better,' said Maximilian.

Then Willow put her paw on top of Maximilian's. 'I want to make it better too,' she said.

And Wilton put his paw on Willow's.

And Lewie put his on Wilton's and Erica put hers on Lewie's and Elvira put her paw on top of Erica's. 'We *all* want to make it better,' she murred with a smile.

Then one small, delicate paw was placed on the top of the pile. 'We're family,' said Mother Tawny-Tail. 'Whatever happens, through thick and thin, we stick together.'

And Shylo knew that they really did.

The following morning, the Royal Rabbits came to find Shylo. It was exactly one week since Shylo had left The Grand Burrow and time for them all to return to London.

'It's time to go, Shylo,' said Laser.

'Yes, back to the, er - beetroot farm,' added Clooney with a grin.

'You are coming with us, *non?*' asked Belle de Paw hopefully. She had seen how much fun Shylo had been having with his family at the party the night before, and now couldn't be sure if he'd changed his mind about being a Royal Rabbit and decided to stay.

Shylo turned to his family.

Maximilian looked at him. 'We want you to stay,' he murred and Shylo's heart swelled with happiness.

'We all do,' added Erica.

'But you're a MONSTER!' boomed Zeno. 'We need monsters like you at the pal– on the beetroot farm,' he corrected.

Shylo knew then that his heart would always be here, on the farm, but he was needed in The Grand Burrow. And it was a good feeling to be needed.

'I must go with them,' he told his family. 'I have work to do and I like the work very much.' He put his hand on his heart. 'But I'll take you all with me, in *here*.'

Mother Rabbit brushed away a tear. She was so proud of her smallest.

Horatio put a paw on the little bunkin's shoulder. 'Well, I'm not going anywhere. I'm home now,' he growled softly. 'When I saw my old books, I realized how much I'd missed them.'

Shylo's mother smiled at the thought of having

Horatio nearby, for she had enjoyed sitting in his warm burrow, listening to his stories about the rise and fall of the Great Rabbit Empire.

After saying their goodbyes to Horatio and Shylo's family, the Royal Rabbits made their way out of the Warren, towards the farm where Mr Ploughman was loading up his van of vegetables. Shylo's heart was heavy because he was leaving his family, but excited too at the thought of the adventures to come.

'Hey, Shylo!'

Shylo turned, surprised to see Maximilian catching up with them.

'How will we find you ... if we need your help again?' Maximilian asked.

Shylo grinned. 'Under the willow tree,' he murred. 'Next to Buckingham Palace.'

'That's a very strange place for a beetroot farm,' said Maximilian suspiciously.

'It's a long story,' Shylo replied. He gave his brother a mysterious smile, and then a quick hug before he hopped off to join the other Royal Rabbits of London.

Maximilian scratched his head and wondered whether Shylo wasn't really part of something very exciting and very secret. Something that he very much hoped his little brother would tell him about one day . . .

# EPILOGUE

It was dark in the earth beneath the Hollow, the natural valley where the Elders of the Warren held important meetings, but the mole didn't notice because she couldn't see much anyway. She was shuffling along, digging her tunnel and sniffing the soil for worms and grubs.

Suddenly, she bumped into something hard. She recoiled in surprise and rubbed her nose. That hurt! When her snout had stopped smarting, she gave the hard thing a sniff.

*Hmmm*, it wasn't what she was looking for, which was the root of the beech tree which led up to a heap of silage on Farmer Ploughman's farm. Silage was full of delicious creatures for Mole to eat. She gave the object a tap with her claw. It sounded solid. She pulled a box of matches out of her pocket and struck one. In the glow of the flame, she could see that the strange, hard thing was gold in colour. She scratched away the earth with her claw, revealing more of it. Goodness, it was big. *Very* big. She wondered for a moment what it could be. But only for a moment because, as it didn't smell of something delicious to eat, she really wasn't very interested.

'Drat!' she exclaimed crossly, blowing out the match. 'Wrong turning!'

And, with that, she left the Golden Carrot where it had been buried for nearly two thousand years and continued digging her tunnel in the direction of of the beech tree and the sumptuous feast that awaited her there.

# ACKNOWLEDGEMENTS

With our deepest thanks to Jane Griffiths, Kate Hindley, Jenny Richards, Jenny Glencross, Sheila Crowley, Luke Speed and Georgina Capel.

Hop over the
page for
some
Royal
Rabbits
extras!

# TOP LEGENDS

The legend of the Golden Carrot plays a big role in this Royal Rabbits adventure. In the story, nobody could quite agree whether or not it really did exist, but the Royal Rabbits certainly believed in it enough to want to try and make sure that troublesome Harlequin would never get his hands on it. Here are some other popular mysteries and myths from around the world:

## Blackbeard's Treasure

From 1716-1718, history's most famous pirate, Blackbeard, and his ship, Queen Anne's Revenge, prowled the West Indies and the Atlantic coast of North America, attacking ships and stealing gold, silver and other treasures. In late 1718 Blackbeard was captured and killed, but before he died he claimed to have hidden his massive treasure and refused to reveal where. Treasure hunters have been searching for it ever since.

# The Loch Ness Monster

The Loch Ness Monster, or Nessie, is a creature said to live in Loch Ness, in the Scottish Highlands. It first gained widespread fane in 1933, when construction began on the A82, the road that runs along the north shore of the loch. The work involved lots of drilling and blasting and it's thought that the disruption forced the monster into the open. Since then many locals and tourists have claimed to see something in the water. However, despite occasional reports, doctored photos and scientific investigations (using everything from submarines to sonar beams), no one has ever been able to prove that the creature exists. Though no one has proved for certain that it doesn't exist either...

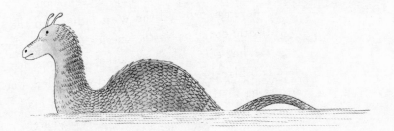

# King Arthur

The legends of King Arthur have captured imaginations for centuries. King Arthur was said to have defended his country against Saxon invaders in the late 5th and early 6th centuries, and he is at the centre of numerous stories. One of the most famous stories about King Arthur is the legend of the Sword in the Stone. Only the person fit to rule England could pull the sword Excalibur from the stone in which the wizard Merlin placed it, and when Arthur did this at the age of fifteen, he was crowned King of England. However, the details of Arthur's life are mainly composed of stories and folk tales, and modern historians disagree about whether he ever actually existed.

# The Holy Grail

The Holy Grail is traditionally thought to be the cup that Jesus Christ drank from at the Last Supper and that one of his followers, Joseph of Arimathea, used to collect Jesus's blood at his crucifixion. Legend says that the Grail has the power to heal all wounds, deliver eternal youth and grant everlasting happiness. The Grail has been the subject of stories and films and books for many centuries, but no one has ever been able to uncover the real thing.

# Shylo's Favourite Corn and Barley Stew Recipe

## Ingredients - serves 4

2 garlic cloves, finely chopped
1 small onion, finely chopped
1 carrot, peeled and chopped
600ml chicken or vegetable stock
200g pearl barley
teaspoon dried sage
Small tin sweetcorn
Small bunch fresh parsley

1. Using a wide-based pan with a lid, ask an adult to help you fry the onion, garlic and carrots together in a splash of oil for 5-10 minutes, or until the carrots are starting to soften.

2. Add the pearl barley, sage, stock and season with salt and pepper. Mix well.

3. Put the lid on the pan and simmer for approx. 40 minutes, stirring every so often to make sure the barley isn't sticking to the bottom of the pan. If it starts to stick, add a little more hot water to loosen it.

4. When the barley is tender, stir in the sweetcorn and parsley and continue to cook for another 10 minutes.

5. Serve and enjoy!

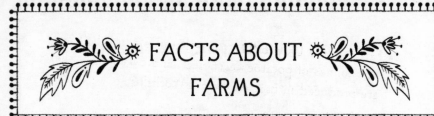

# FACTS ABOUT FARMS

Farmer Ploughman and his wife are forever chasing the rabbits away from their crops. And while Shylo and his family need to eat, the Ploughmans also need to protect their farming business, because farms play an important role in the UK. Here are a few facts about farms:

- There are around 280,000 farms in Britain.

- Farmland covers around 60 per cent of the UK with more than 20 million hectares of land - that's the same as 30 million football pitches.

- 60% of all food eaten in the UK is grown on British farms.

- Wheat is the most common crop in the UK, with over two million hectares harvested every year.

- Farms in the UK produce more than five and a half million tonnes of potatoes each year, and over half of these are produced in East Anglia and Yorkshire.

- Barley, oats, cereal, carrots, beans, cabbages, pears and apples are some of the other popular crops produced in the UK.

- Every day, British farms supply 20 million eggs and the grains to make nine million loaves of bread.

- Arable farms produce crops, such as wheat and vegetables (like Farmer Ploughman and his wife), while pastoral farms raise animals for meat, wool or dairy products. Mixed farming is when a farm grows crops as well as keeping animals.

- Crops have been farmed by people to eat for thousands of years. Archaeologists have found evidence of the first signs of farming as long ago as 12,000 years.

Have you read
Shylo's other adventures?

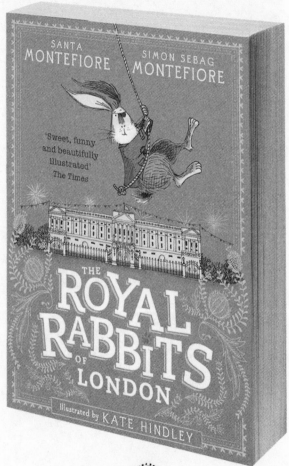

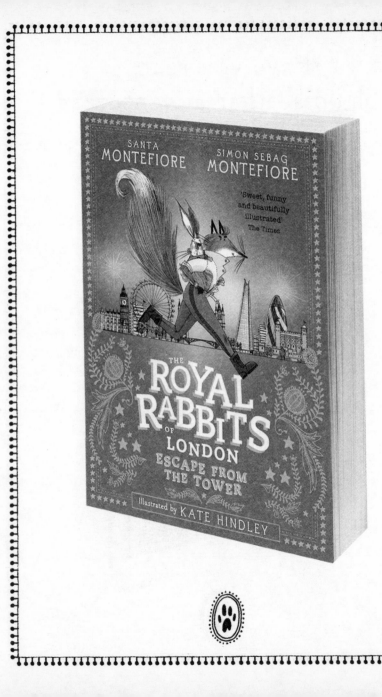

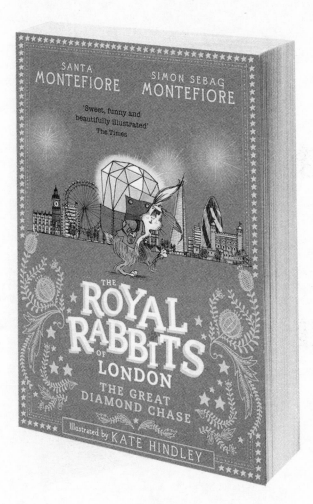

SANTA
MONTEFIORE

SIMON SEBAG
MONTEFIORE

'Sweet, funny and
beautifully illustrated'
The Times

# THE
# ROYAL
# RABBITS
## OF LONDON
### THE GREAT
### DIAMOND CHASE

Illustrated by KATE HINDLEY

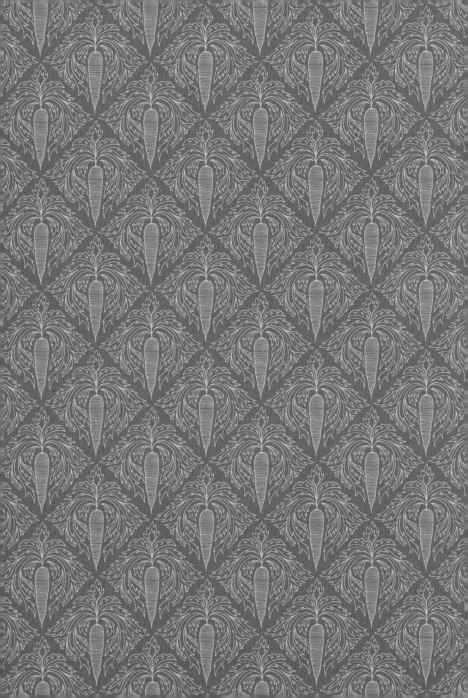